The Bride of the Sun

BY THE SAME AUTHOR

The Phantom of the Opera
Rouletabille and the Mystery of the Yellow Room
Rouletabille at Krupp's (2013)
Cheri-Bibi (stage play)

Gaston Leroux

The Bride of the Sun

Translated and introduced by
Jean-Marc & Randy Lofficier

A Black Coat Press Book

ISBN 978-1-64932-038-4. First Printing. January 2021. Published by Black Coat Press, an imprint of Hollywood Comics.com, LLC, P.O. Box 17270, Encino, CA 91416.

Introduction

L'Épouse du Soleil was originally serialized in the magazine *Je Sais Tout* Nos. 86 (March 1912) to (August 1912), then collected in book form by Pierre Lafitte in 1913.

The leading *feuilletoniste* of the Belle Époque was Gaston Leroux (1868-1927), a writer best known for his classic *Le Fantôme de l'Opéra* (1910),[1] the tragic yet murderous man-ape *Balaoo* (1911), and the adventures of *Chéri-Bibi*, a man unjustly pursued by a hostile fate (1913, 1919).[2]

Trained as a lawyer, Leroux was a renowned investigative journalist who even traveled to, and reported from, Russia just before the Bolshevik Revolution. His journalistic skills helped the French *fantastique* emerge from the melodramatic and romantic literary burdens of the end of the 19th century, and, by making it more real and contemporary, gave it a new lease on life.

In *The Phantom of the Opera*, Leroux skillfully mixed fantastic events with real-life facts. The same was true of *Le Fauteuil Hanté* [*The Haunted Chair*] (1909), a fantastic mystery novel in which a mad scientist used

---

[1] Black Coat Press, 978-1-932983-13-5.
[2] Stage play adaptation, Black Coat Press, 978-1-934543-43-6.

ingenious, murderous devices to rid himself of appli-
cants at the French Academy who have uncovered his
dark secret. Both novels read like sensational newspaper
accounts of the surreal.

Leroux's eclectic curiosity conferred upon his *oeu-
vre* a wildly diverse nature. In his first novel, *La Double
Vie de Théophraste Longuet* [*The Double Life of
Theophraste Longuet*] (1903), a retired merchant found
himself possessed by the spirit of notorious 18th century
French highwayman, Cartouche. He goes on to discover
a secret, underground society which has been living in
vast caverns beneath Paris since the 14th century.

Later, Leroux shied away from purely supernatural
themes, with a few exceptions: short stories such as the
Hoffmannesque *L'Homme qui a Vu le Diable* [*The Man
Who Saw The Devil*] (1908) and *Le Coeur Cambriolé*
[*The Burglared Heart*] (1920).

When Leroux dealt with such fantastic themes, it
was in ways that were resolutely modern, but often de-
rivative of the works of other popular writers. His classic
Balaoo (1911) was about a murderous ape-man *à la* Ed-
gar Allan Poe's *Murder in the Rue Morgue*. *L'Épouse du
Soleil* [*The Bride of the Sun*] (1912) was a Lost World
story with pure H. Rider Haggard elements. Finally, *La
Poupée Sanglante* [*The Bloody Puppet*] (1923) and *La
Machine à Assassiner* [*The Killing Machine*] (1924)
were a strange combination of classic horror and science
fiction. In the first volume, the brain of Benedict Mas-
son, a man framed for murder and later guillotined, is
transplanted into the body of Gabriel, an android. In the
sequel, Gabriel exposes a vampire cult–one without
some of the more supernatural characteristics usually
associated with vampirism–led by a depraved nobleman.

Leroux's literary idols being Alexandre Dumas and Paul Féval, the author of the seminal *The Black Coats* series, it was no surprise that he was equally comfortable chronicling extravagant tales of murder, revenge, masked men, swooning women, mysterious dwarves and secret societies meeting in underground caverns, with or without fantastic elements. Like their American pulp counterparts of the 1930s, these sagas were fantastic more in terms of their atmosphere than because of any specific supernatural concepts. In this vein, the ever-prolific Leroux penned *Le Roi Mystère* [*King Mystery*] (1908), a *Count of Monte-Cristo*-like story, *La Reine du Sabbat* [*The Queen of the Sabbath*] (1910) and *Les Mohicans de Babel* [*The Mohicans of Babel*] (1926), which both owe a clear debt to *The Black Coats*.

Leroux also wrote *Les Aventures Effroyables de Herbert de Renich* [*The Terrifying Adventures of Herbert de Renich*] (1917-20), an epic undersea saga which was his answer to Verne's *Twenty-Thousand Leagues Under the Sea* in which a Captain Nemo-like American designs a super-submarine to fight the Germans who are responsible for the death of his family. In chapter 7, the narrator, de Renich, says, speaking of the new generation of submarines: "they do things the *Nautilus* couldn't do... After all, that was only a ship... They, on the other hand, also drive at will on the bottom of the sea. Yes, they have wheels and can be either ships or vehicles."

Today, Gaston Leroux is best remembered as the author of a series of mystery novels starring the character of dashing young journalist, Joseph Josephin, a.k.a. Rouletabille, clearly an idealized projection of the author, and conceived as a direct challenge to Conan Doyle. Like C. Auguste Dupin, Lecoq, Sherlock Holmes and Hercule Poirot, Rouletabille solved his cases by pure deductive reasoning, what he called the "good end of reason." He drew a figurative circle around the facts that were known, and excluded everything that was not part of that circle, even if, to others, they appeared to be.

The Bride of the Sun appears to have strongly inspired cartoonist Hergé when he write and drew his classic *Tintin* story of *The Temple of the Sun*, first published in the comic magazine *Tintin* in 1946.

Indeed, Hergé copies many elements from Leroux's novel, the main one being the plot. In both cases, a relative of the hero is kidnapped by men who are descendants of the Incas. They live in a "lost city" where they perpetuate their culture in secret, centuries after their bloody defeats at the hands of the Conquistadores. (This place evokes the mythical city of Vilcabamba, the last Inca city to resist the European invaders.)

The myth of the lost Inca city, inhabited or not, but unknown to the rest of the world, has left a strong mark on the Western imagination, as these two masterpieces of popular fiction prove.

Jean-Marc Lofficier

THE BRIDE OF THE SUN

BOOK I: THE GOLDEN SUN BRACELET

CHAPTER I

As the liner steamed into Callao Roads, and long before it had anchored, it was surrounded by a flotilla of small boats. A moment later, deck, saloons and cabins were invaded by a host of gesticulating and strong-minded boatmen, whose badges attested that they were duly licensed to carry off what passengers and luggage they could. They raged impotently, however, around Monsieur François-Gaspard Ozoux, the worthy member of the Institute, Department of Inscriptions and *Belles-Lettres*, of Paris, who sat enthroned on a pile of securely locked boxes in which were stored his cherished manuscripts and books.

It was in vain that they told him it would be two full hours before the ship came alongside the Darsena dock. Nothing would part him from his treasures; nothing would induce him to allow these half-crazed foreigners to hurl his precious luggage overside into those frail-looking skiffs.

When this was suggested to him by a tall, handsome young man who called him "uncle," the irascible Academician explained with fluency and verve that the idea was an utterly ridiculous one. So Raymond Ozoux shrugged his broad shoulders, and with a "See you soon" that hardly interrupted his uncle's flow of words, beckoned to a boatman.

A moment later, the young man had left the ship's side and was nearing the shore—the Eldorado of his ambition, the land of gold and legends, the Peru of Pizarro and the Incas. Then, the thoughts of a young girl's face blotted out those dreams to make way for new ones.

The monotonous outline of the waterfront brought no disappointment. Little did Raymond care that the city stretched out there before his eyes was little more than a narrow, unbeautiful blur along the sea coast, that there were none of those towers, steeples or minarets with which ancient ports beckoned out to sea that the traveler was welcome. Even when his boat had passed the Mole, and they drew level with the modern works of the Muelle Darsena, well calculated to excite the interest of an engineer like him, Raymond remained indifferent.

He had asked the boatman where the Calle de Lima lay, and his eyes hardly left the part of the city which had been pointed out to him in reply. At the landing, he threw a hand-full of *centavos* to his man, and shouldered his way through the crowd of guides, interpreters, hotel touts and other waterside parasites.

Soon, he was before the Calle de Lima, a thoroughfare which seemed to be the boundary line between the old city and the new. Above, to the east, was the business section—streets broad or narrow fronted with big, modern buildings that were the homes of numerous English, French, German, Italian and Spanish firms. Below, to the west, was a network of tortuous rows and alleys, full of color, with colonnades and verandas encroaching on every available space.

Raymond plunged into this labyrinth, shouldered by muscular Chinese carrying huge loads, and by watchful natives. Occasinally, one would notice a sailor leaving or entering one of the many cafés which opened their doors into the cool bustle of the narrow streets. Though it was his first visit to Callao, Raymond hardly hesitated. Then he stopped short against a decrepit old wall close to a veranda from which came the sound of a fresh young voice—young but very assured.

"Just as you like, señor," it said in Spanish. "But at that price, your fertilizer can only be of an inferior quality."

For a few minutes, the argument went on within. Then there was an exchange of courteous farewells and a door was closed.

Raymond approached the balcony and looked into the room. Seated before an enormous ledger was a young girl, busily engaged in transcribing figures into a little notebook attached by a gold chain to the daintiest of waists. Her face, strikingly beautiful, was a little set under its crown of coal-black hair as she bent over her ledger. It was not the head of a Southern belle—rather the curls of a Carmen, a blue-eyed Minerva, a goddess of reason and a thorough business-woman.

At last she lifted her head.

"Marie-Thérèse?"

"Raymond!"

The heavy green ledger slipped and crashed to the floor, as she ran toward him, both hands outstretched.

"How is business?"

"So, so… And how are you? I did not expect you until tomorrow."

"We made a rather good time."

"How is Louise?"

"She's quite grown-up now. I suppose you've heard? Her second baby was born just before we left."

"And dear old smoky Paris?"

"It was raining hard when last I saw it."

"Where is your uncle?"

"Still on board. He won't leave his collection... Does nothing all day but take notes for his next book... Wait a minute, I'll come in. Where's the door? I suppose it would be bad form to climb in through the window? Won't I be in the way, though? You seem awfully busy..."

"I am, but you may come in. Round the corner there, and the first door on your right."

He followed her indications and found an archway leading into a huge courtyard crowded with Chinese coolies and Quichua Indians. A huge dray, coming from the direction of the harbor, rumbled under the archway, and wheeled in the court to let an empty one pass out. People and things seemed to unite in making as much dust and noise as possible.

So she manages all this, he reflected as he made his way toward a door at which she had appeared.

"You may kiss me," she said as she closed the door behind them.

He took her in his arms and held her to him, by far the more troubled of the two. Again it was she who spoke first.

"So you really have not forgotten?"

"Could you believe it, darling?"

"Well, you were so long in coming..."

"But I wrote, and..."

"Well, never mind now. It is not too late. I have just turned down my fourth suitor, Don Alfonso de Cuellar. And father, I think, is furious with me for refusing the most eligible young man in Lima... Well, why don't you say something?"

"Forgive me, darling... How is your father? I hardly know what I am saying..."

"Father is very well, and very glad to hear that you were coming. To tell the truth though, he is far more interested in your uncle's visit. He has arranged a meeting at the Geographical Society for him. And for the past month he has been thinking and talking of nothing but archaeology. They have been digging up all kinds of things."

"And so, he has been angry with you?"

"He seems to think he has every reason to be. I am twenty-three and he already sees me as an old maid... It's awfully funny! Do you know what they call me in Lima now? The Bride of the Sun!"

"What does that mean?"

"Aunt Agnes and Aunt Irene will explain better than I can. It's something like one of the Vestals—an old Inca legend."

"Hum, some superstitious rot, no doubt... But you know, Marie-Thérèse, that I'm an awful coward. Do you think that your father..."

"Of course! He'll do anything I like if he is asked at the right moment We'll be married in three months' time at San Domingo. Truly we will!"

"Darling! But I'm only a poor devil of an engineer, and he may not think much of me as a son-in-law for the Marquis de la Torre."

"Nonsense, you're clever, and I'll make you a gift of the whole of Peru. There's plenty to do here for an engineer."

"I can hardly believe my luck, Marie-Thérèse! That I... But, tell me, how did it all happen?"

"The old, old way. First, you are neighbors, or meet by accident. Then, you are friends... just friends, nothing else... And then...?"

Their hands joined, and they remained thus for a moment, in silence.

Suddenly, a burst of noise came from the courtyard, and a moment later, a hurried knock announced the entrance of an excited employee. At the sight of the stranger, he stopped short, but Marie-Thérèse told him to speak. Raymond, who both understood and spoke Spanish well, listened.

"The Indians are back from the Islands, señorita. There has been trouble between them and the Chinese. One coolie was killed and three were badly wounded."

Marie-Thérèse showed no outward sign of emotion. Her voice hardened as she asked:

"Where did it happen? In the Northern Islands?"

"No, at Chincha."

"Then Huascar was there?"

"Yes, señorita. He came back with them, and is outside."

"Send him in."

CHAPTER II

The man left, gesturing as he went to a stalwart Indian who walked quietly into the office.

Marie-Thérèse, back at her desk, hardly raised her eyes. The newcomer, who took off his straw sombrero with a sweep worthy of a hidalgo, was a Trigullo Indian. These are perhaps the finest tribe of Peru and claim descent from Manco-Capac, first king of the Incas. A mass of black hair, falling nearly to his shoulders, framed a profile which might have been copied from a bronze medallion. His eyes, strangely soft as he looked at the young girl before him, provoked immediate antagonism from Raymond. He was wrapped in a bright-colored poncho, and a heavy sheath-knife hung from his belt.

"Tell me how it happened," ordered Marie-Thérèse without returning the Indian's salute.

Under his rigid demeanor, it was evident that he resented her tone, especially in front of a stranger. But he began to speak in Quichua, only to be interrupted and told to use Spanish. The Indian frowned and glanced haughtily at the listening engineer.

"I am waiting," said Marie-Thérèse. "So your men have killed one of my coolies?"

"The shameless ones laughed because we fired *cohetes* in honor of the first quarter of the Moon."

"I do not pay your men to pass their time in setting off fireworks."

"It was the occasion of the Noble Feast of the Moon."

"Yes, I know! The moon, and the stars, and the sun, and every Catholic festival as well! Your men do noth-

15

ing but celebrate. They are lazy, and drunkards. I have tolerated this so far because they were your friends, and you have always been a good servant, but this is too much."

"The shameless dogs of China are not your servants. They do not love you..."

"No, but they work hard."

"For next to nothing... They have no pride."

"They earn their wages... Your men, on the other hand, I keep mostly out of charity!"

"Charity!"

The Indian stepped back as if struck, and his hand, swung clear of the poncho, was lifted over his head as if in a gesture of menace. Then it dropped and he strode to the door. But before opening it, he turned around and spoke rapidly in Quichua, his eyes flaming. Then, throwing his poncho over his shoulder, he went out.

Marie-Thérèse sat silent for a while, toying with her pencil.

"What did he say?" asked Raymond.

"That he was going, and that I shall never see him again."

"He looked furious."

"Oh, he is not dangerous. It is a way they have. He says he did everything he could to prevent the trouble... He is a good man himself, but his gang are hopeless. You have no idea what a nuisance these Indians can be. They're proud as Lucifer, but lazy as drones... I shall never employ another one."

"Wouldn't that make trouble?"

"It might! But what else can I do? I can't have all my coolies killed off like that."

"And what of Huascar?"

"He will do as he pleases... He was brought up in this house, and was devoted to my mother."

"It must be hard for him to leave."

"I suppose so."

"And you wouldn't do anything to keep him?"

"No... Goodness me, we are forgetting all about your uncle!" She rang, and a man came in. "Order the car... By the way, what are the Indians doing?"

"They left with Huascar."

"All of them?"

"Yes, señorita."

"Without saying a word?"

"Not a word, señorita."

"Who paid them off?"

"They refused to take any money. Huascar ordered them to."

"And what of the coolies?"

"They have not been near the place."

"But the dead man... and the wounded?"

"The Chinese took them back to their own quarters."

"Funny people... Tell them to bring the car around."

While speaking, she had put on a bonnet, and now drew on her gloves.

"I shall drive," she said to the servant who brought the car.

As they shot toward the Muelle Darsena, Raymond admired the coolness with which she took the machine through the twisting streets. The servant, crouching at their feet, was evidently used to the speed, and showed no terror as they grazed walls and corners.

"Do you do a great deal of motoring out here?"asked Raymond.

"No, not very much. The roads are too bad. I always use this to get from Callao to Lima, and there are one or two runs to the seaside, to places like Ancon or Carillos—just a minute, Raymond..."

She stopped the car, and waved her hand to a curly gray head which had appeared at a window, between two flower pots. This head reappeared at a low door, on the shoulders of a gallant old gentleman in sumptuous uniform. Marie-Thérèse jumped out of the motor, exchanged a few sentences with him, and then rejoined Raymond again.

"That was the Chief of Police," she explained. "I told him about that affair. There will be no trouble unless the Chinese initiate legal proceedings, which is not likely."

They reached the steamers' wharves in time. The tugs had only just brought alongside the Pacific Steam Navigation Company's liner, on board which Uncle Franços was still taking notes:

"On entering the port of Callao, one is struck, etc., etc."

He lost precious material by not being with Marie-Thérèse as she enthusiastically described "her harbor" to Raymond... Sixty millions spent in improvements... 50,000 square meters of docks... How she loved it all for its commercial bustle, for its constant coming and going of ships, for its intense life, and all it meant—the riches that would flow through it after the opening of the Panama Canal... the rebirth of Peru... Chili conquered and Santiago crushed... the defeat of 1878 avenged... and San Françoisco yonder had best look to itself!

Raymond, listening to the girl at his side, was amazed to hear her give figures with as much authority as an engineer, estimate profits as surely as, a ship owner. What a splendid little brain she had, and how much better than that imaginative, dreaming type which he deplored both in men and women, a type exemplified by his uncle with all his chimerical hypotheses.

"It would all be so splendid," she added, frowning, "if we only stopped making fools of ourselves. But we are always doing it."

"In what way?"

"With our revolutions!"

They were now standing on the quay, while the liner gradually swung in.

"Oh, are they at it here as well? There was one in Venezuela, and then another at Guayaquil. The city was under martial law, and some general or other who had been in power for about forty-eight hours was preparing to march on Quito and wipe out the government."

"Yes, it is like an epidemic," replied the young girl, "an epidemic which is sweeping the Andes just now. The news from Boloisa is worrying me, too. Things are bad around Lake Titicaca."

"Really? That's a nuisance... not a cheerful outlook for my business in the Cuzco."

Raymond was evidently put out by the news.

"I had not intended telling you about it until tomorrow. You must not think of unpleasant things today... all that district is in the hands of Garcia now."

"Who is he?"

"Oh, one of my old suitors."

"Has everybody in the country been in love with you, Marie-Thérèse?"

"Well, I had the attraction of having been brought up abroad... at the first presidential ball I went to after mother's death, there was no getting rid of them... Garcia was there. And now he has raised a revolt among the

Arequipa and Cuzco Indians... He wants Vointemilla's place as president."

"I suppose they have sent troops against him?"

"Oh, yes, there are two armies out there... but, of course, they are not fighting."

"Why?"

"Because of the festival of the Interaymi."

"What on earth is that?"

"The Festival of the Sun... You see, three quarters of the troops on both sides are Indian... So, of course, they get drunk together during the fêtes... In the end, Garcia will be driven over the Boloisan border, but in the meantime, he is playing mischief with fertilizer prices..."

She turned toward the liner again, and, catching sight of Uncle François, raised her hand in reply to the frantic waving of a notebook.

"How are you, Monsieur Ozoux?" she cried. "Did you enjoy the crossing?"

The gangways were run out, and they went on board.

François Ozoux's first question was the same as had been his nephew's.

"I'm well. How is business?"

All those who had known her in France couldn't help but marvel at the change which had come over the "little girl" after her mother's death, when she had suddenly decided to return to Peru and take charge of the family's fertilizer business and concessions. She had also been influenced in this decision by the fact that there were her little brother and sister, Isabella and Christobal, who needed her care. And finally, there was her father, perhaps the greatest child of the three, who had always lavishly spent the money which his wife's business had brought in.

Marie-Thérèse's mother, the daughter of a big French ship owner, had met the handsome Marquis de la Torre one summer when he was an attaché at the Peruvian legation in Paris. The following winter, she had gone back to Peru with him. Inheriting a great deal of her father's business acumen, she had made a great success of a guano concession which her husband had hitherto left unexploited.

At first, the Marquis had protested vigorously that the wife of Christobal de la Torre should not work, but when he found that he could draw almost any sums of money from an ever-replenishing bank account, he had forgiven her for making him so wealthy. Yet, on his wife's death, he had not been surprised that Marie-Thérèse had inherited her abilities, and had allowed her to take over all her duties.

"Where is your father, my dear?" asked Uncle François, still with a wary eye on his luggage.

"He did not expect to see you until tomorrow. They are going to give you such a reception! The whole Geographical Society is turning out in your honor."

When his luggage had been taken to the station, and he had personally supervised its registration for Lima, Uncle François at last consented to take a seat in the car, and Marie-Thérèse put on full speed, for she wished to reach home before the early tropical nightfall.

After passing a line of adobe houses and a few comfortable villas, they came to a long stretch of marshy ground, overgrown with reeds and willows, and spotted with clumps of banana trees and tamarisks, with an eucalyptus or an araucaria pine here and there. The whole countryside was burnt yellow by the sun, by a drought hardly ever relieved by a drop of rain, which made the campo round Lima and Callao anything but enchanting. A little further along, they passed some scattered bamboo and adobe huts.

This parched landscape would have been infinitely desolate had it not been relieved at intervals by the luxuriant growth surrounding some hacienda—sugar-cane, maize and rice plantations, making a brilliant green oasis around the white farm buildings. The badly-built clay roads which crossed the highway were peopled by droves of cattle, heavy carts, and flocks of sheep which mounted shepherds were bringing back to the farms. All this animation formed a strange contrast to the arid aspect of the surrounding country. Despite the jolting shaking of the car over a poorly kept road, Uncle François kept taking notes, and even more notes. Soon, with the lower spurs of the Cordilleras, they saw on the horizon the spires and domes which made Lima look almost like a Muslim city.

They were now running alongside the Rimac, a stream infested by crayfish. Native fishermen were to be seen every few yards dragging behind them in the water sacks attached to their belts, in which they threw their catch to keep it alive. Turning to comment on them, Raymond noticed Marie-Thérèse's preoccupied air, and asked her the cause.

"It is very strange," she said, "we have not met a single Indian."

The car was almost in Lima now, having reached the famous Ciudad de los Reyes, the City of Kings founded by the Conquistadors. Marie-Thérèse, who loved Lima, and wished to show it off, made a detour, swerving from the road and running a short distance along the stony bed of dried-up Rimac, careless of the risk to her tires.

Certainly, the picturesque corner to which she brought them was worth the detour. The walls of the houses could hardly be seen, overgrown, as it were, with wooden galleries and balconies. Some of them were for all the world like finely carved boxes, adorned with a hundred arabesques—little rooms suspended in mid-air, with mysterious bars and trellised shutters, and strongly reminiscent of Bagdad. Only here, it was not rare to see women's faces half-hidden in the shadows, though in no way hiding. For the ladies of Lima were famed for their beauty and coquetry. They were many in the streets, wearing the manta, that fine black shawl which is wrapped around the head and shoulders and which no woman in South America uses with so much grace as the women of Lima. Like the *haik* of the Moors, the manta hides all but two great dark eyes, but its wearer can, when she wishes, throw it aside just enough to give a sweet glimpse of harmonious features and a complexion made even more clear by the provoking shadow of the veil. Raymond had this amply proved to him, and seemed so interested that Marie-Thérèse began to scold him.

"They are far too attractive in those mantas," she said. "I shall show you some European neighborhoods now."

She turned the car up an adjoining street, which brought them to the new city, to broad roads and avenues opening up splendid vistas of the distant Andes. They crossed the Paseo Amancaes, which is the heart of Lima, and Marie-Thérèse several times exchanged bows with friends and acquaintances. Here the black manta was replaced by Parisian hats ordered from the Rue de la

Paix. It was the hour at which all fashionable Lima was driving or walking, or gossiping in the tearooms, where one loiters happily over *helados* in an atmosphere of chiffons, flirting and politics.

When they reached the Plaza Mayor, the first stars had risen on the horizon. The crowd was dense, and carriages advanced only at a walking pace. Women dressed as for the ball, with flowers in their dark curls, passed in open carriages. Young men grouped around a fountain in the center of the square, raised their hats and smiled into passing victorias.

"It really is strange," murmured Marie-Thérèse, "not an Indian in sight!"

"Do they generally come to this part of the city?"

"Yes, there are always some who come to watch the people walk by..."

Standing in front of a café was a group of half-breeds, talking politics. One could distinctly hear the names of Garcia and Vointemilla, the president, neither of them treated over gently. One of the group, evidently a shopkeeper, was moaning his fears of a return to the era of *pronunciamentos*.

The car turned at the corner of the cathedral, and entered a rather narrow street. Seeing the way clear, Marie-Thérèse put on speed only to pull up sharply a second later, just in time to avoid running down a man wrapped in a poncho, who stood motionless in the middle of the street. Both young people recognized him.

"Huascar!" exclaimed Marie-Thérèse.

"Huascar, señorita, who begs you to take another road," said the man.

"The road is free to all, Huascar. Stand aside."

"Huascar has nothing more to say to the señorita. To pass, she must drive over Huascar."

Raymond half rose in his seat, as if to intervene, but Marie-Thérèse put a hand on his sleeve.

"You behave very strangely, Huascar," she said. "Why are there no Indians in the town today?"

"They do as they please; they are free men."

She shrugged her shoulders, thought a moment, and began to turn the car around. Before starting again, however, she spoke to the Indian, who had not moved.

"Are you still my friend, Huascar?"

For his answer, the Indian slowly raised his sombrero, and looked up to the early stars, as if calling them to witness. With a brief "Adios!" Marie-Thérèse drove on.

When the car stopped again, it was before a big house, the door-keeper of which rushed out to help his young mistress to alight. He was forestalled, however, by the Marquis de la Torre himself, who had just driven up, and who greeted the two Frenchmen with delight.

"Enter, señor. This house is yours," he said grandly to Uncle François.

The Marquis was a slim little gentleman of excessive smartness, dressed almost like a young man. When he moved, and he was hardly ever still, he seemed to radiate brilliancy: from his eyes, his clothes, his jewels. But for all that, he was never undignified, and kept his grand manner without losing his vivacity in circumstances when others would have had to arm themselves with severity. Outside his club and the study of geographical questions, he cared for nothing so much as romping with his son Christobal, a sturdy youngster of seven. At times, one might have taken them for playmates on a holiday from the same school, filling the house with their noise, while little Isabella, who was nearly six, and loved ceremony, scolded them pompously, after the manner of an Infanta.

CHAPTER III

The Marquis de la Torre's residence was half-modern, half-historical, with here and there quaint old-fashioned rooms and corners. Don Christobal was something of a collector, and had adorned his home with ancient paneling, carved galleries several centuries-old furniture dating back to before the Conquest, faded tapestry—all so many relics of the various towns of old Peru which his ancestors had first sacked and then peopled. Each object recalled some anecdote or story which the host detailed at length to all willing listeners.

It was in one of these historical corners that Monsieur Ozoux and his nephew were presented to two old ladies—two Velasquez canvases brought to life, yet striving to retain all their pictorial dignity. Attired after a fashion long since forgotten, Aunt Agnes and her duenna might almost have been taken for antiques of Don Christobal's collection: they lived altogether in another age, and their happiest moments were those passed in telling fear-inspiring legends. All the tales of old Peru had a home in this ancient room of theirs, and many an evening had been whiled away there by these narratives—the two Christobals, father and son, and little Infanta Isabella listening in one corner, while Marie-Thérèse, at the other end of the room, went over her accounts and wrote her letters in a great splash of yellow lamplight.

Uncle François was delighted to meet in real life two such perfect types of the New Spain of yore, set in the very frame they needed. They were great friends at once, and the savant, taken to his own room, changed his

26

clothes hurriedly to be able to rejoin them. At dinner, installed between the two, he begged for more legends, more stories. Marie-Thérèse, thinking it was time to talk of more serious matters, interrupted by telling her father of the trouble between the Indians and the Chinese coolies.

When they heard that Marie-Thérèse had discharged the Indians, Aunt Agnes shook her head doubtfully, and Irene openly expressed her disapproval. Both agreed that the young girl had acted imprudently, and particularly so on the eve of the Interaymi festival. This view was also taken by the Marquis, whose protest took an even more active form when he learned that Huascar had also left. Huascar had always been a very faithful servant, he argued, and his brisk departure was strange. Marie-Thérèse explained shortly that, for some time past, Huascar's manner had displeased her, and that she had let him know it.

"That is another matter," said the Marquis.

"But I am no more comfortable about it... There is something in the air... The Indians are not behaving normally... The other day, in the Plaza Mayor, I heard extraordinary remarks being made by some half-breeds to a couple of Quichua chiefs."

"Yes, we did not meet a single Indian on the way from Callao, and I have not seen one in the city," said Raymond. "Why is that, I wonder?"

"Because of the festival," interjected Aunt Agnes. "They have their secret meetings. They disappear into the mountains, or some warren of theirs—catacombs, like the Early Christians. One day, the order comes from some corner of the Andes, and they vanish like shadows, to reappear a few days later like a swarm of locusts."

"My sister exaggerates a little," said the Marquis, smiling. "They are not so very dangerous, after all."

"But you yourself are worried, Christobal. You have just said so."

"Only because there might be some rioting..."

"Have they got it in them?" asked Monsieur. Ozoux. "They seem so placid..."

"They are not all like that... Yes, we have had one or two native rebellions, but it was never anything very serious."

"How many of them are there in the country?" put in Raymond.

"About two-thirds of the population," answered Marie-Thérèse. "But they are no more capable of really rebelling than they are of working properly. It is the Garcia business that has unsettled them, coming after a long period of quiet." She turned to her father. "What does the President think of it all?"

"He does not seem to worry a great deal. This Indian unrest recurs every ten years."

"Why every ten years?" demanded Uncle François.

"Because of the Sun Festival," said old Irene. "The Quichuas hold it every ten years."

"Where?" Raymond took a sudden interest.

"Nobody knows," replied Aunt Agnes, in a nervously strangled voice. "There are sacrifices... and the ashes of the victims are thrown into rivers and streams... to carry away the sins of the nation, the Indians believe."

"That is really very interesting!" exclaimed Uncle François.

"Some of the sacrifices are human," half-groaned the old lady, dropping her head to her plate.

"Human sacrifices!"

"Oh, Auntie!" laughed Marie-Thérèse.

"Curious," remarked the savant. "And there may be some truth to it. I know that they were customary at the Festival of the Sun among the Incas. And Prescott makes it clear that the Quichuas have kept not only the language of their ancestors, but also many of the ancient customs."

"Yes, but they became Christians when the Spaniards conquered their country," suggested Raymond.

"Not that that affects them much," commented the Marquis. "It gives them two religions instead of one, and they have mixed up the rites and beliefs of the two in a most amazing fashion."

"What do they want to do, then? Rebuild the Inca Empire?"

"They don't know what they want," replied Marie-Thérèse. "In the days of the Incas, every living being in the Empire had to work; they were practically the slaves of the Sons of Sun. When that iron discipline was removed, they gradually learned to do nothing but sleep. Of course, that meant poverty and misery, which they attribute, not to their laziness, but to the fact that they are no longer ruled by the descendants of Manco-Capac! From what Huascar told me, they still hope for a return of the old kings."

"And they still go in for human sacrifice?" asked Raymond.

"Of course not! What absolute nonsense!" Aunt Agnes and Irene both turned to Uncle François.

"Marie-Thérèse was brought up abroad, and does not know... She cannot know... But she is wrong to laugh at what she calls 'all these old stories.' There is plenty of proof, and we are sure of it... Every ten years—all great events were decennial among the Incas—every ten years, the Quichua Indians offer a bride to the Sun."

"A bride to the Sun?" exclaimed Uncle François, half-horrified, half-incredulous.

"Yes... they sacrifice a young girl in one of those horrible Inca temples of theirs, where no stranger has ever gone! It is terrible, but true."

"Really? It is so difficult to believe... Do you mean to say that they kill her?"

"They do... as a sacrifice to the Sun."

"But how? By fire?"

"No, it is even more horrible than that. Death by fire is only for far more unimportant ceremonies. At the Interaymi, they wall up their victim alive... And it is always a Spanish girl! They kidnap one, as beautiful and of as good family as possible. It is their vengeance against the race that destroyed them."

Marie-Thérèse was frankly laughing at her aunt's intense seriousness, only equaled by gravity with which Uncle François listened. The savant looked at her smiling face half-disapprovingly, and brought his scientific knowledge to the defense of the old ladies. Everything they said corresponded perfectly with what well-known writers and explorers had been able to discover about the Brides of the Sun. There was no doubt that human sacrifice had been rife among the Incas, both in honor of the Sun and for the King himself, many of the victim» going to the altar of their own free will. This was particularly the case when an Inca King passed away.

"Prescott and Wiener, the greatest authorities on the subject, all agree," said Uncle François. "Prescott tells us that at one royal burial, more than a thousand people, wives, maids and servants of the Inca, were sacrificed on his tomb."

Aunt Agnes shuddered, while Irene, bending her head, made the sign of the Cross.

"All this is very true, my dear Professor," said Don Christobal, carrying on the conversation, "and I see that our Geographical Society here will be able to give you very little that is new to you. Would it interest you to visit our latest excavations at Ancon tomorrow? There is ample proof there that such sacrifices were practiced among the Incas."

"What exactly were these Brides of the Sun?" asked Raymond, turning to his uncle, who, delighted to be able to show his erudition, at once launched into an explanation.

"The Brides of the Sun, or Chosen Ones, as they were called, were young girls, sworn to the service of their divinity. They were taken from their families as children, and put into convents where they were placed under the care of women called *mammaconas*—girls who had grown old in these monasteries. Under the guidance of these venerable matrons, the virgin brides were taught their religious duties; weaving and embroidery were their chief occupations, and it was they who made the fine vicuna wool for the hangings of the temples and the Inca's home and attire."

"Yes," said gray-haired Irene, "but their chief duty was to guard the sacred fire acquired anew by the temple at each Raymi festival."

"That is so," replied the savant. "They lived absolutely alone. From the moment they entered these convents, they were entirely cut off from their families and friends. Only the Inca king, and his queen, the Coya, were allowed within the sacred precincts. The most rigid discipline and supervision were exercised over them."

"And woe to the girl who transgressed," added Aunt Irene. "By Inca law, she was buried alive, while the town or village from which she came was razed to the

31

ground and sown with stones, so that all memory of it should be lost."

"You are perfectly right, Madame," agreed Uncle François.

"What a sweet country!" Raymond exclaimed.

"What an amazing civilization they must have possessed," continued Uncle François. "The ceremonies of their temples are almost identical with those of ancient Rome... Little did Christopher Columbus think, when he saw a few painted savages, that on the other side of the ocean, behind this belt of primitive land and tribes, there was a whole world with its customs, monuments, laws and kings. Two empires, in fact: that of the Aztecs in Mexico, that of the Incas in Peru. And with civilizations rivaling that of the Mediterranean Basin. It is as if an Eastern prince, reaching the steppes of Scythia, had claimed the discovery of Europe, returning to his States without knowing that Rome existed, and convinced that the rest of the world was a howling waste!"

"He must have been a bit of a fool," hazarded Raymond. "A true conqueror guesses there are new lands to conquer even before he sees them."

"Like Pizarro and Cortes!" exclaimed the Marquis.

"Who came to destroy everything..." began Uncle François.

Fortunately, Don Christobal did not hear him, and he stopped in time. Marie-Thérèse, seated opposite the savant, had trodden on his foot, and he bit his lip, remembering that de la Torre, the Marquis' ancestor, had been one of Pizarro's "destroyers."

Both old ladies, however, had heard, and opened their eyes at this denunciation of a cause which, to them, was that of the true faith against the infidel. Marie-

Thérèse, anxious to smooth matters over, quickly brought them back to their Inca legends.

"All this is very fine," she said, "but there is nothing to show that the Indians still sacrifice human beings."

"How can you say that!" they exclaimed in chorus.

"Well, has anybody ever had definite proof of it?"

Aunt Agnes was not to be shaken in her convictions.

"When I was a little girl," she declared, "I had an old nurse who belonged to one of the Lake Titicaca tribes of Quichuas. She told me that she herself had seen three Spanish girls walled up alive at three successive Interaymi fêtes."

"Where did the girls come from?" asked Raymond.

"They were Lima girls."

"But then, any number of people must have known of it," he observed, secretly amused by the grave airs of the two old ladies.

"It was, and is, common knowledge," retorted Aunt Agnes. "The names of their last two victims were known to everybody. One vanished ten years ago, and the other ten years before that."

"Yes, yes, common knowledge!" laughed Don Christobal.

"There is nothing to laugh about, Christobal," said Aunt Agnes drily.

And the duenna repeated in a low voice:

"No, no, nothing to laugh about."

The Marquis was determined to have his laugh.

"Let us mourn the poor children," he said, groaning. "Cut off from the affection of their parents at so early an age! How terrible!"

"Christobal, can you tell me what became of Amelia de Vargas and Marie Cristina de Orellana?"

"Yes, what became of them?" urged Irene.

"There we are! The old story! I expected it!" exclaimed the Marquis.

"You might speak seriously! You knew Amelia de Vargas..."

"A charming girl... the sweetest smile in the city! That was twenty years ago... How time flies!... Yes, she disappeared... with a poor cousin of hers."

"I heard the other day that it was a toreador," interjected Marie-Thérèse. "They revive that old story every ten years, at the time of the Interaymi."

"She disappeared outside the bull ring," explained Aunt Agnes. "There was a fight in the crowd, and she was separated from her parents. Nobody ever saw her again. Afterwards, some people remembered catching sight of her surrounded by a group of Indians. She died at their hands, walled up alive."

"What a gorgeous imagination crowds have! But the fact remains that that poor cousin of hers disappeared at about the same time."

"So you are pleased to say, Christobal. But what of Maria Cristina de Orellana?"

"Oh, that was another matter... a very sad case. She was out for a walk with her father round the Cuzco, and went into one of the caves, never to reappear. She lost her way in the old subterranean passages, of course. The government had all the entrances blocked up after that."

"And since then," commented Aunt Agnes, "her poor father has been a madman. For the past ten years, he has haunted the Cuzco ruins, calling in vain to his daughter. He will not believe that she was not carried off by the Indians."

"But you yourself said he is mad."

"He lost his reason when he acquired the certitude that she had perished in their temple. A few days before she vanished, Maria-Cristina mysteriously received a very old and heavy gold bracelet. That bracelet had a central motif representing the sun..."

"My dear Agnes, you know that in this country jewelers stick the sun on wherever and whenever they can."

"That bracelet was the real one... the same one that was sent to Amelia."

"Aren't you exaggerating a little, Agnes? Really? And with stories like these running about, they expect poor historians to be accurate! I hope you 're not taking notes of all this, Monsieur Ozoux?"

"I am exaggerating nothing," retorted Aunt Agnes obstinately. "It was the real Golden Sun bracelet... Every ten years since Atahualpa, the last Inca king to be burned alive by Pizarro, the Inca priests have sent it to a Spanish girl they had chosen to be the Bride of the Sun. And every one of them has been walled up alive... I remember that poor Orellana girl laughing and joking about the Golden Sun bracelet! The whole town knew about it."

"The whole town always have a pretty lively imagination at the time of the Interaymi," insisted the Marquis. He turned to Monsieur Ozoux. "You have no idea, my dear Professor, how hard it is for our Society to get away from all these weird legends."

"Legends are not things to be despised in research work," disagreed Uncle François. "For my part, I am delighted to have found a country where they are still so much alive."

At this moment, a servant came in with a small parcel on a silver tray.

"A registered package, señorita," he said. "Will the señorita sign here?"

Marie-Thérèse, having signed, was turning the box over in her hand.

"It is from Cajamarca," she remarked. "Who from, I wonder? I know nobody there. Will you excuse me?"

The young girl cut the string, broke the seals and opened the little wooden box.

"A bracelet!" she exclaimed, and laughed a little nervously. "What an extraordinary coincidence! Why, it is the Golden Sun bracelet! It really is! The bracelet of the Bride of the Sun!"

Every person in the room had risen, with the exception of the two old ladies, who sat there, stunned. All eyes were turned on the heavy bracelet in darkened old gold, with its sun-adorned center motif on which the rays appeared blurred out by the dust of centuries.

"Well, that is funny!" laughed Marie-Thérèse.

"Of course!" exclaimed the Marquis, whose voice had changed a little. "Evidently a joke by Alfonso de Cuellar. You refused him, my dear, and he has come up with a rather petty revenge—his little vengeance on the Bride of the Sun... All the young men in town call you that because you've refused to marry any of them... Well, what are we looking so blue about over there? Surely, Agnes, you are not going to make yourself ill over a harmless joke like this?"

Marie-Thérèse was showing the bracelet to Uncle François and Raymond.

"Father!" she exclaimed. "I think I shall keep it! Tell Don Alfonso I shall wear it as a token of friendship... It really is beautiful! What do you think of it, Monsieur Ozoux?"

"It seems to me at least three or four hundred years-old."

"Pieces like that are still occasionally found in excavations around royal tombs, but they are rare," said the Marquis. "I am not surprised Don Alfonso had to go to Cajamarca for that one."

"Where is Cajamarca?" asked Raymond.

"Cajamarca," said the savant, horrified by his nephew's ignorance, "is the Caxamarxa of the Incas, their second capital in Pizarro's day..."

"And the city where their last king was burned at the stake!" groaned Aunt Agnes.

They rushed to her side, for she was on the point of fainting and had to be carried to her room. The old duenna followed them, as white as her lace, and crossing herself tremulously.

CHAPTER IV

On the day after his arrival, Uncle François was solemnly and officially received by the Geographical Society of Lima, the fine archeological, statistical and hydrographical work of which keenly interested him. With so much scientific enthusiasm, he conquered all hearts. By far the proudest and happiest man present, however, was Don Christobal, basking in the reflected glory of his distinguished guest. As they were all leaving after the ceremony—Marie-Thérèse wearing her bracelet despite the protests of her aunt and the duenna—the Marquis met Don Alfonso de Cuellar.

"Why, Cuellar," he exclaimed, "I thought you were at Cajamarca!"

Don Alfonso opened his eyes in surprise, evidently not understanding.

"Come, come, Cuellar, you may confess. I shall not be angry. Both Marie-Thérèse and I agree that your little revenge was a very neat one."

"What revenge?"

"The bracelet, of course!"

"What bracelet?"

At this moment, Marie-Thérèse and Raymond joined the group. Marie-Thérèse, seeing her father laughing as he talked, felt quite sure that the mystery of the bracelet had already been cleared up.

"Thank you ever so much," she said, holding out the slim hand adorned by the heavy bracelet "You see, I wear it as a token of friendship."

"But I should never have permitted myself such a liberty," protested the young man, looking in amazement from one to the other.

"Are you serious? It really was not you?"

"No! What does it all mean? And what a peculiar bracelet."

"Don't younot recognize it?" laughed Marie-Thérèse, still unconvinced. "It is, apparently, the Golden Sun bracelet which the Indian priests always send to the Bride of the Sun at the Interaymi... And as you, I understand, were the originator of my nickname, I naturally supposed that, despite everything you heard, you bore no malice to me."

"What a charming idea! I am only sorry," he added, "that it was not mine. I shall never forgive myself for not having thought of it. You must attribute it, señorita, to one of those other unfortunates who, like myself, have worshiped you in vain... There is Pedro Ribera... He looks dark enough to have done it... Ribera!"

But Ribera knew no more of the bracelet than Don Alfonso. He also admired the strange bracelet, and was equally sorry that he had not sent it.

Don Christobal was becoming irritated, and was sorry now that he had mentioned the matter to them. He could not, without appearing ridiculous, ask them not to speak of it, and he knew very well that, within two hours, every café table in the Plaza Mayor would be discussing the new topic. Marie-Thérèse guessed his thoughts.

"As our guess was wrong, the whole thing rather loses its point So we must wait until the generous donor comes and confesses. In the meantime, let it be forgotten."

And, slipping off the bracelet, she put it into her reticule.

"I wonder if it was Huascar," suggested Raymond, as the two young men left.

"Huascar? Why Huascar?" asked the Marquis.

"Well, it's an old Indian bracelet... He's the only Indian I know of, and I know he is very devoted to the family. Suppose he found the bracelet in some old ruin and didn't know what to do with it...?"

"Oh, let us not talk of it anymore," interrupted Marie-Thérèse, slightly troubled. "What does it matter! Besides, we are bound to know, sooner or later... Someday, a friend of father's, back from the Sierra, will ask me why I am not wearing his present. That is sure to happen."

"Of course it is," affirmed Raymond.

The Marquis, far from satisfied, and still seeking a possible explanation, suddenly turned on Raymond.

"You sent it!" he exclaimed, triumphant.

"I? Why, I have only just arrived in the country..."

"But you could very well have bought it when the liner stopped at Guayaquil, and then sent it to some agent or other at Gajamarca to have it forwarded here... You must have read the legend of the bracelet in one of your uncle's books."

"Really, Father!" protested Marie-Thérèse. "Monsieur Ozoux is an engineer..."

"Yes, yes, I know. Very hard-working... Here to try experiments with some new pump to clear the Cuzco gold mines of water... I know all that... But that is no reason why he should not have sent you that bracelet."

"But why should he, Father?"

"Is there a reason why he should not, my daughter?"

This time, Marie-Thérèse blushed deeply and Raymond tried to look unconcerned, while Don Christobal smiled at them quizzically.

"So you thought your old father was blind, eh? You Thought he guessed nothing... that he did not understand what you had left behind in Paris?... Well, Raymond?"

"Really, sir... I... I... hardly dared hope..."

"Didn't you? There, there, that's enough... You may put the bracelet on her arm again... What a pair of young fools."

Marie-Thérèse slipped her arm through her father's, and squeezed it.

"Dear Father!"

Then, turning to Raymond and opening her reticule, she whispered rapidly:

"Say that you sent it. What can it matter?"

Raymond, completely taken aback, clasped the bracelet on Marie-Thérèse's wrist without protest. He scarcely heard a word said by the Marquis, who was delighted to have solved the mystery.

"Well, young man, you can flatter yourself that you thoroughly mystified everybody."

And with that he hurried after Uncle François, who had been carried off to drink champagne by a group of admirers.

Raymond and Marie-Thérèse, left alone, exchanged a look. A moment later, they were brought to earth again by the advent of a horde of excited scientists.

"But what will your father say when he finds out who really sent the bracelet?"

"He will forgive you. I only made you tell the story to reassure him. Between you and me, those old tales told by Aunt Agnes and Irene were worrying him a little... He is rather a child in some ways."

Carriages and automobiles were rapidly filling with people starting for the excavations outside the town, and then on by rail to Ancon, where Uncle François was to be shown the latest Inca discoveries. The Marquis and Monsieur Ozoux passed them in one car. Marie-Thérèse waved to them, and walked on towards the town with Raymond.

They were all to meet again that evening to dine and pass the night at the Marquis' seaside villa between Lima and Ancon. Uncle François would thus be able to begin his researches the very next morning, for Don Christobal's villa, itself a treasure trove of antiques, stood in the very center of the excavations.

Meanwhile, the young people, less interested in dead things than the members of the Geographical and Archaeological Society, went to explore Lima. It was only after a long walk in the Pascos de Amancaes that they, in turn, started by car over an execrable road.

The approach of night could already be felt, and the great plain over which they were speeding was made even more desolate by the presence of the slow-flying gallinazos, or black vultures, overhead. These scavengers, half-starved in appearance, are the common adjuncts of scenery in Peru, tolerated and even respected, as they are, by a grateful municipality.

Here and there were haciendas, each with its group of pastures and grazing horses, kept from galloping into the surrounding waste by the four-foot mud walls. Otherwise, it was a sandy desert, at some points dotted with skeletons of a long-dead species dug up by curious scientists and then left to bleach in the sun.

"Not exactly cheerful," commented Raymond.

Marie-Thérèse, intent on her driving, did not answer, but pointed with one gloved hand at a group of half-breeds playing bowls with human skulls at the corner of a hacienda.

They were soon in the outskirts of Ancon, and found the Marquis, Uncle François, and their fellow-scientists busily arguing in the center of an Inca cemetery. On all sides were opened tombs, each containing a mummy rudely drawn from its thousand-year sleep by the pick of the excavator. Raymond and Marie-Thérèse had left their motor, but did not join the others. Instead, they wandered silently, almost sadly, in another direction, and the car had started off again in the care of the negro chauffeur, to be garaged at Ancon.

"It is horrible," said Marie-Thérèse, pressing Raymond's hand. "Why can't they leave them in peace?"

Seated on a little mound well out of sight of the others, they forgot their surroundings. And it was in this horrible burial-ground they exchanged their first true lovers' kiss.

The sound of voices brought them back to reality. The president of the Society, followed by an interested retinue, was explaining the most interesting tombs.

"Walking through this necropolis," he said, "it is no effort to evoke the shades of the Incas, and to feel for a minute as if one were living among them... Here, six feet below ground, we first found a dog which had been sacrificed on its master's tomb... The dead man's wife and chief servants also followed him to the next world... We next found the wife's body... Like the dog, she had been strangled, probably because she had not had the courage to take her own life... Finally, we heard the Indian workman cry out, '*Aqui esta el muerto*' (Here is the dead one) for, to the native mind, the only body worthy of notice is that of the master... When we cut the thongs and unrolled the wrappings about him—the man had evidently been a great chief—we found the mummy in an extraordinary state of preservation,—the head was almost intact... Gentlemen, the ancient Egyptians did no better."

At this moment, excited sounds from another part of the cemetery attracted their attention. A workman ran up to tell them that a sensational discovery had just been made—the tomb of three Inca chiefs with strange-shaped skulls. Raymond and Marie-Thérèse followed the others to the spot in question.

When they reached the newly-discovered tomb, workmen were passing up to the surface little sacks full of corn, jars which had once contained *chicha*—all the things necessary for a long voyage in the afterworld. Then came golden-vases, silver amphora, goblets, hammered statuettes, jewels:—a veritable treasure brought to light by one stroke of the pick. Finally, the three mummies were brought to the surface and unrolled with every precaution. One of the scientists present bent down to uncover the faces, and there was a murmur of horror from those present.

To understand what Raymond and Marie-Thérèse had been among the first to see, it is necessary for the reader to know that it was customary among the Incas to shape living skulls to any form they wished. This strange custom still exists even in modern days, though in a far lesser degree, among the Basque inhabitants of the Pyrenees. The skulls of babies, set in vices or bound into various molds, were gradually deformed until they took the shape of a sugar-loaf, of a squarish box, of an enormous lime, and so forth. Phrenology was evidently a science known to the Incas, who, precursors of Gall and Spezhurn, thus sought to develop abnormally the intellectual or warlike qualities of a child by compressing or enlarging such and such part of his brain. It has been proved, though, that this practice was allowed only in the case of children of the Inca himself, called upon in afterlife to take a high position. The common people kept their normal skulls and normal brains.

Of the three heads just brought to light, one was cuneiform—a monstrous sugar-loaf. It was horrible to see this nightmare face, like the head of a beast of the Apocalypse, framed in locks which seemed to be still living as they gently moved in the sea breeze. The second head was flattened out, cap-like, with a huge bump at the back. The third was almost square, resembling nothing so much as a small suitcase.

Marie-Thérèse shrank before this triple horror and, despite his evident curiosity, drew her fiancé away from the violated sepulcher. They strolled down to the beach, where the Pacific murmured gently as it came to rest on the sands. So peaceful is the sea at Ancon, so free from currents and gales, that it has become the great beach resort for the inhabitants of Lima. At this season, however, it was still deserted, so that Raymond and Marie-Thérèse met nobody during their walk to the Marquis' villa.

It was dusk when they reached it, still under the depressing influence of the three strange heads, and vainly trying to joke the impression away. As the sun disappeared on the horizon, the wind rose and conjured up in the half-light pale sand whorls which might have been so many phantoms dancing up from the huacas to reproach them for impiety and sacrilege. Though they were neither of them overly imaginative, they were glad to see the fat majordomo who came forward to announce that the Marquis and Uncle François had already arrived. He, at least, was solid flesh and blood.

As Marie-Thérèse entered the house, a little Quichua maid, Concha, literally threw herself at her mistress' feet, protesting that she had been dead in the señorita's absence, and had been brought to life again by her return.

"See what devotion we get here for eight *soles* a month!" she laughed, completely cured of her fears by the sight of the familiar objects about her. "Into the bargain, she cooks *puchero*, our native stew, to perfection. You must try it someday."

"Señorita," interjected the maid, her broad lips parting in an enormous smile, "I have prepared *locro* for tonight."

Dinner was not a very long meal. Everybody was tired, and Uncle François was anxious to be up early in the morning. Raymond and Marie-Thérèse prosaically enjoyed their *locro*—maize cooked with meat, spiced and served with the *chicha* which still further heightens the taste of all popular dishes in Peru—and, when they parted at the doors of their rooms on the first floor, they were quite ready to laugh over the incidents of the afternoon. Marie-Thérèse's hand lingered in Raymond's.

"Good night, my little Bride of the Sun," he said, and bending down, kissed the disk on the bracelet. "But surely you are not going to keep that thing on? A bracelet from Lord knows where and from Lord knows whom?"

"It is dear to me now, Raymond. Now that you have kissed it, it shall never leave me. Good night."

She disappeared into her room, and the young engineer had already turned toward his when a shriek was heard. Marie-Thérèse had rushed back to the landing, in a panic.

"They are in there! They are in there!" she gasped, her teeth chattering.

"What? What is the matter?"

"The three living skulls!"

"Marie-Thérèse!"

"I tell you they are! All three of them, staring in through the window! They looked at me with such eyes... horrible, living eyes... No, no! Raymond!... Don't go in!"

Taking the light from her trembling hand, Raymond went into the room. There was nothing to be seen. He crossed to the balcony, and threw open the French windows; on one side was the sea, on the other a panorama over the flat country and the Inca burial-ground. Everything was perfectly normal.

"Come, darling... You must have imagined it..."

"Raymond, I tell you I saw them!"

"What did you see?"

"There, on the balcony, staring through the panes... Those three Inca chiefs with their hideous heads."

"But, Marie-Thérèse, be reasonable. They are dead... You yourself saw them being dug up... Surely, you cannot believe in ghosts..."

"Those I saw were not ghosts. They were alive!"

Trying to reassure her, he began to laugh heartily.

"Don't, Raymond, don't!" she said. "I did see them... They were exactly like those in the grave... the sugar-loaf, the cap, and the suitcase... Exactly the same! But what did they come here for?"

Don Christobal, drawn from the smoking room by the noise, jeered at his daughter's fears. Uncle François, too, appeared in a nightcap, which started everybody laughing except Marie-Thérèse. To quieten her, the majordomo was sent outside and explored the grounds. He returned to report that he had found nothing.

"You are worried by what you saw this afternoon, my child," said the Marquis.

But Marie-Thérèse would not reenter the room, and ordered another one, on the opposite side of the villa, to be prepared for her. Raymond, using every argument he could think of, finally convinced her that she had been the victim of a hallucination. Half-ashamed of herself, she made him go out to the first floor balcony with her, trying, in her turn, to erase any unfavorable impression she might have made.

The balcony on which they stood was almost directly over the sea, for on this side of the house, the beach reached right up to the walls of the villa. After a time, the immense peace of the night completed Raymond's work, and the girl was perfectly quiet when she took off her bracelet.

"I think this is what has been worrying me," she said. "I never before imagined that I saw a ghost..."

And she threw the bracelet into the sea.

"A very good place for it," agreed Raymond. "A ring will do ever so much better. And you will know where it comes from."

Before long, the whole house was at rest, and the remainder of the night passed by quietly. But at seven o'clock, when people were beginning to stir again, an agonized scream from Marie-Thérèse's room sent the servants rushing to her aid. When they entered the room, they found their mistress sitting up in bed, staring at her wrist with horror-stricken eyes.

The Golden Sun bracelet had mysteriously returned during the night!

BOOK II: THE LIVING PAST

CHAPTER I

Raymond was nearly as frightened as Marie-Thérèse when he found what had happened. On the previous night, he himself had seen her throw the bracelet into the sea, and yet, there it was on her arm again when she'd woken up. What could it all mean? He could find nothing to say, and in spite of himself, began to go over the terrible legend told by the two old ladies. It was preposterous, impossible, but now, he could not help believing in it.

The Marquis and Uncle François, brought out by the noise, joined the others in the young girl's room. Don Christobal's sharp voice drove the servants from the room and brought out the whole story. Raymond confessed his duplicity in the matter of the bracelet, and told how the jewel had been thrown away.

Marie-Thérèse was shaking with fever, and her father took her in his arms. He was less worried by the strange story she'd just told him than by the state in which she was. He had always seen her so calm, so sure of herself, that her new-found terror shook all his own convictions.

As to Uncle François, half-pleased with this striking story for his next book, he could only repeat:

"But it's impossible, you know. Quite impossible."

And then, it was all explained in the most absurdly obvious way. Little Concha, back from marketing at Ancon, hurried to her mistress' room and brought the solution of the mystery with her. Childishly naive, she explained that, on going out onto the beach in the morning, she had seen something glitter in the sand. She picked the object up, and found that it was a bracelet, which she recognized as the one worn by her mistress on the previous day. Thinking that it had accidentally fallen from the balcony, and rushing to give Marie-Thérèse a pleasant surprise, she had put it back on her arm without waking her. A huge burst of laughter from them all greeted the end of her simple story and Concha, terribly vexed, ran out of the room.

"It seems to me we are all getting a little mad," said the Marquis.

"That infernal bracelet is enough to drive one to a lunatic asylum," added Raymond. "We must get rid of it at all costs."

"No! If it ever came back a second time, I could not answer for my reason." said Marie-Thérèse, joining nervously in the laughter. "What we all need," she added, "is a change of air, of scenery... We ought to go for a little trip in the mountains, Father, and show a little of our country to Monsieur Ozoux and Raymond... Suppose we start tonight? Back to Lima first, and not a word to Aunt Agnes or Irene, for it would make them both ill... I shall go into Callao with Raymond to give a few orders, and in the evening, we'll take the boat."

"To get to the mountains?"

"Of course, Father. To get to Pacasmayo."

"Pacasmayo!" groaned the scientist "A horrible place. I know it. Our liner put in there for four hours.

There's nothing interesting in that part of the world, is there?"

"Nothing interesting! Why, do you know where one goes to from Pacasmayo? To Cajamarca, Monsieur Ozoux!"

Uncle François straightened himself up:

"Cajamarca! The Caxamarxa of the Incas!"

"The very place."

"Cajamarca... The dream of my life, my dear!"

"There is nothing to prevent it becoming a reality. And at the same time, Father, we can find out the name of the mysterious sender of this thing. It was sent from Cajamarca, you remember?"

"An excellent idea," agreed Don Christobal. "We really must find a solution to that mystery."

"And whoever the joker is, he will pay for it," said Marie-Thérèse, who was now toying with the bracelet. "He laughs best who laughs last!"

With that, she drove them all out of her room and called for Concha, who, when she came to dress her mistress, received a masterly box on the ears to teach her to wake people up next time she brought back a lost bracelet. Concha, unused to such treatment, burst into tears, and Marie-Thérèse, ashamed of herself, filled the little maid's hands with chocolates to make her smile again. But do what she would, Marie-Thérèse could not regain her calm. Every movement she made betrayed the inward storm, and she stamped whenever she thought of the cowardice she had shown...

Broadly speaking, all roads in Peru are little more than mule-paths. The only exception is in favor of the great paved highways built by the Incas, which link the wilds of Bolivia to the capital of Ecuador, and in comparison with which the finest monuments of the Gallo-

Roman period are not so very remarkable, after all. It is for this reason that travelers wishing to reach the interior must take a boat along the coast to one of the harbor towns which are the termini of the railways leading into the ever-delightful Sierra.

For Peru may be divided into three great parallel bands of country. First ,the Costa, or coast district, which rises gradually from sea level to an altitude of 1500 to 2000 meters on the western slopes of the Andes. Then, the Sierra, half-mountain and half-plateau, with altitudes varying between 2000 and 4000 meters. Finally, the Montaña, with its forests, which sweeps down to the east of the Cordilleras, stretching toward the Amazon in long slopes which, from 2000 meters, gradually drop to only 500. Landscape, climate and products are all different in these three zones. The Costa is rich; the Sierra has smiling valleys and a relatively warm climate; the Montaña is a veritable ocean of verdure.

Perhaps the most curious thing in this curious country is the variety of its landscape in a relatively small region; for to reach the Sierra, one is obliged to scale some of the highest mountains in the world, and that in an equatorial country. In a few hours, one travels through districts where trees of all latitudes and plants of all climates grow and are cultivated side by side. Walnut-trees neighbor with waving palms; beetroot and sugar-cane grow in adjoining plantations; here, an orchard full of splendid apples; there, a group of banana-trees spreading their broad leaves to the sun. In this amazing country, landowners can offer their guests drinks cooled with ice from the hills just above and made with sweet limes picked in the tropical gardens around the house.

Uncle François was in raptures, brimful of enthusiasm, and so schoolboyish in his delight that his companions could not help laughing. They teased the old gentleman constantly, and once, the hiding of his fountain-pen at a moment when the taking of notes was urgent made him nearly frantic. All, in short, were in the best of spirits, and seemed to have completely forgotten the Golden Sun bracelet. This had been left in the care of Aunt Agnes and Irene, who immediately took it to the church of San Domingo and left it as an offering on the altar of the Lady Chapel.

There was an exciting landing for the travelers at Pacasmayo. They got ashore with the aid of an enormous raft, rising and falling with the waves alongside the liner. This raft, they reached by means of a cradle swung out on a small crane. All one had to do was to wait until the raft rose to within jumping distance of the cradle.

Marie-Thérèse led the way, and landed very neatly on her feet; the Marquis, used to such gymnastics, followed suit; and Raymond reached the raft with his hands still in his pockets. Uncle François, thinking hard of something else, arranged his own descent so badly that raft and cradle met with a crash which nearly jerked him into the sea. The shock was forgotten in a wave of enthusiasm over the novelty of it all, and he even retained his equanimity when the jerk of the grounding raft sent him rolling onto the wet sand of the beach.

It was not until the following morning that the party left Pacasmayo, without any untoward incident disturbing the peace of a journey commenced under the most favorable auspices.

Raymond was the only one to think twice of the advent of a coppery-colored gentleman who seemed to have attached himself to their party. Had he not worn European dress, the stranger might well have passed for a typical Trujillo—that Indian race of which Huascar was certainly the finest representative. On the other hand, he wore his lounge suit with ease, and during the voyage, evidenced his civilized upbringing by rendering to Marie-Thérèse several of those little services which a man may allow himself to do when traveling, even to a woman he does not know. The stranger had embarked at Callao, had landed by the same raft as they, had stopped at the same inn in Pacasmayo, and, the following morning, took the same train for Cajamarca.

They were so engrossed with the landscape of the lower ranges of the Andes that they did not at first notice his presence in their carriage. He drew their notice to himself in such an unexpected manner that all, without knowing exactly why, experienced a strange feeling of discomfort.

There had been a chorus of exclamations and interjections over the variety of the panorama before them, and they had just entered the wildest gorge imaginable, when the stranger said in a grave voice:

"Do you see that camp, señores? That is where Pizarro's first messengers reached the last King of the Incas."

All turned at the words. The stranger, standing at the back of the observation platform, seemed to see nobody; with arms crossed, he stared out toward the rocky fastnesses at the foot of which the world's greatest adventurer had rested for a moment before starting on the conquest of an Empire.

"One of my ancestors was there!" exclaimed the Marquis involuntarily.

"We know it! We know it!" said the stranger, without turning, and in such a voice that the others exchanged astonished glances. His statuesque immobility also had its effect on them. Then after a moment's silence, he continued:

"No, we have not forgotten that a Christobal de la Torre was with Pizarro. We know the whole story, señor. When Pizarro left the Spanish colony of Panama, vaguely guessing that before him was an empire even greater than the one which Cortes had just given to Charles V, when, after a thousand dangers, he saw himself on the point of being deserted by all, he drew his sword and, with the point, drew a line in the sand from east to west. Then, turning toward the south, he said:

" 'Comrades, on this side are danger, privation, hunger, nakedness, ruin and death; behind us, comfort and mediocrity. But to the south are also Peru and its riches, glory and immortality. Let each one decide for himself which is best for a hidalgo of Castille!'

"And with those words, he crossed the line. He was followed by Ruiz, his brave pilot, then by Pedro de Candia, a knight born, as his name shows, in one of the Greek islands. Eleven others crossed that line, ready to follow their chief to the world's end. And among those eleven was Juan-Christobal de la Torre. We know it! señor, we know it!"

"And, pray, who are you, señor?" demanded the Marquis brutally, exasperated by the stranger's manner, though he had in truth remained studiously polite.

As if not hearing, as if intent on doing homage to the exploits of those dead Conquistadors, the stranger continued:

"Is there not, señores, is there not, señorita, something gigantic in this spectacle? This little handful of men confidently starting on an expedition as wild as the wildest deeds of their knights-errant, a handful of men, señores, without clothes or food, almost without arms, left by their comrades on a deserted mountainside to start on the conquest of one of the most powerful empires ever known. And among those men, there was a Christobal de la Torre... Señor Don Marques, it is a glorious descent to claim... And allow me to present myself: I am your servant, Huayna Capac Buntu, head clerk of the Franco-Belgian Bank of Lima... But we may fittingly travel in company, señor, for I am of royal blood. Huayna Capac, King of the Incas, who succeeded his father at the age of sixteen, married first Pillan Huaco, by whom he had no children. He then took two other wives, Bava-Bello and his cousin Mama-Buntu. I am the descendant of that Huayna Capac and that Mama-Buntu!"

"Now on leave from your bank?" queried the Marquis, almost insolently.

There was a flash in the Indian's eyes as he answered somberly:

"Yes, on leave, for the Interaymi."

Raymond started at these words, already repeated so often in connection with the Golden Sun bracelet. He glanced at Marie-Thérèse, who was evidently ill at ease at the turn taken by the conversation between her father and the stranger. She now remembered him quite clearly as a clerk with whom she had had dealings over a consignment of phosphates for Antwerp. An insignificant little man, she had thought—not at all the haughty Indian of today, discarding the disguise of his European clothes and proclaiming himself for what he was. Knowing by experience how susceptible Trujillos are, and fearing that a careless word from her father might provoke a storm, she intervened:

"The Interaymi! Of course, your great festival. Is it to be particularly celebrated at Cajamarca?"

"This year, señorita, it will be particularly celebrated throughout the Andes."

"But you do not admit outsiders? What a pity... I should so like to see it... One hears so many things..."

"Old wives' tales, señorita," rejoined the Indian, with a complete change of manner.

He smiled, disclosing a line of teeth which Raymond mentally compared to those of a wild animal, and added in a slightly lisping voice:

"There is a lot of nonsense talked... Human sacrifices, and so forth... Do I look as if I were going to such a ceremony? I and my clothes by Zarate? No, señorita, just a few little ceremonies to keep alive the memory of our lost glories... a few pious invocations to the God of Day, a few prayers for poor Atahualpa, our last King, and that is all... At the end of the month, señorita, I shall be back at my bank in Lima."

Reassured by the matter-of-fact level reached by these words, Raymond growled at his own absurd fears. A smile from Marie-Thérèse and a grumbled comment on kings and bank clerks from Uncle François completely dispelled the cloud raised by the mention of the Interaymi.

Their train was now traveling along the bed of a ravine, closed in by dizzying heights. High up above, in a band of blazing blue sky, giant condors could be seen winging their way in heavy circles.

"To think of Pizarro facing country like this!" exclaimed Raymond. "How on earth was it that they were not simply wiped out by the Incas?"

"They came as friends, señor," answered the Indian.

"That is all very fine, but it still does not explain it. How many men were there with Pizarro when he marched on Cajamarca?"

"He had received reinforcements," interjected the Marquis, twisting his mustache, "and there were then a hundred and seventy-seven of them."

"Minus nine," corrected the Indian.

"That is, unless I am mistaken, only a hundred and sixty-eight," put in Uncle François, busy with his notebook.

"Why minus nine?" questioned Marie-Thérèse.

"Because, señorita," replied the descendant of Mama-Buntu, who seemed to know the history of the conquest of Peru better than the descendants of the conquerors themselves, "because Pizarro gave his new followers the same chance to draw back that the others had received. He had halted in the mountains to rest his band and make a careful inspection. As you have said, señor, they were then only a hundred and seventy-seven, including sixty-seven horse. There were only three harquebusiers, and a few crossbowmen—not more than twenty altogether. And with this band, Pizarro was marching against an army of 50,000 men and against a nation of twenty millions! For, under the Incas, Peru included what are today called Peru, Ecuador, Bolivia and Chile. At this point, señores, he decided that his soldiers were still too many. He had noticed that some faces were dissatisfied, and, fearing that the discontent might spread, he decided to cut away the weak limbs before the gangrene reached the main body.

"Marshaling his men, he told them that they had reached a crisis in their fortunes—not a man must go on who doubted its ultimate success. It was still not too late for waverers to return to San Miguel, where he had already left some of his companions. He was prepared to risk all with those who still wished to follow him. Nine men took advantage of Pizarro's offer—four infantrymen and five from the cavalry. The others stayed with their general."

"And cheered him to the echo at the call of Christobal de la Torre, who served the Conquistador like a brother!" exclaimed the Marquis.

"We know, we know!" repeated the clerk.

His tone roused the Marquis again.

"And might I ask why you are pleased to recall all these things?" demanded Don Christobal haughtily.

"To prove to you, señor, that the vanquished know the history of their country even better than the conquerors," retorted Runtu with an emphasis not a little ridiculous in a man of his dress and calling.

"Look! How beautiful!" exclaimed Marie-Thérèse, anxious to divert their attention to the landscape.

Their train was passing over a bridge from which a panorama of unparalleled beauty could be obtained. Before them stretched the giant chain of the Andes, peak heaped on peak. On one side, a rent in the ridges opened onto green forests, broken by little cultivated plateaus, each with its rustic cottage clinging to the rugged mountain-side And there, above, snowy crests sparkling in the sun—a chaos of savage magnificence and serene beauty to be found in no other mountain landscape of the world.

It was almost more terrible than beautiful, and as the train crossed abyss after abyss over quivering bridges, Marie-Thérèse, clinging to Raymond's arm, could not help murmuring:

"And even this did not daunt Pizarro."

Unfortunately, she was overheard by the stranger, who took up the broken conversation with evident hostility:

"We could have crushed them easily, could we not?"

The Marquis, turning superciliously, flicked the questioner's shoulder with his glove:

"And, pray, why did you not do so, then?"

"Because we, sir, were not traitors!"

Raymond had only just time to stop the Marquis, who was on the point of rushing at the insolent Indian. Marie-Thérèse, knowing her father's pride, calmed him in a moment by urging in an undertone that it would be ridiculous for a man of his rank and age to pay more attention to an Indian bank clerk.

"You are quite right," said Don Christobal with a gesture of contempt under which the Indian stood motionless as a statue. He had not been without guessing the sense of Marie-Thérèse's remarks, and might have said more had not the stopping of the train definitely closed the incident.

The railway line, then still in course of construction, went no farther. The remaining thirty miles to Cajamarca had to be covered on mule back, for they were still in the heart of the mountains, and the defiles were steep.

It was too long a journey, however, for the tired travelers to undertake until the following morning. Clinging to the flanks of the rocks were a few rude sheds in which were lodged the men working on the line. Nearby, surrounding a canteen, stood a dozen fairly comfortable tents, in which they themselves were to pass the night In a meager pasture just beyond, some thirty mules wandered at liberty, grazing. Above, the omnipresent galinagas flew in circles against a purple sky.

Dinner, served on the brink of a chasm from which rose the mutter of the racing stream, was a happy meal. Buntu had vanished, and did not reappear until after nightfall, when Marie-Thérèse met him near her tent. He was very apologetic, and, hat in hand, excused himself for the incident in the train. He had had no intention of being rude, and knowing that the Marquis was a great friend of the manager of the Franco-Belgian bank, he hoped that he would not carry the matter further.

Marie-Thérèse, conquering a strong desire to laugh, promised the descendant of the Incas that he would not lose his clerkship through them. When he had bowed himself out of sight, she carried the story to her father and Raymond, who were vastly amused. Then they all went to bed, with the exception of Uncle François, who passed the greater part of the night putting his notes in order and writing an article for a monthly journal in which he re-told the story of the conquest of Peru, with the aid of the Last of the Incas. This Indian he sketched as a gloriously picturesque character, carefully omitting to say that he wore European clothes!

As every night since the appearance of the three strange heads on her balcony, Marie-Thérèse found sleep with difficulty. Tonight, though tired by the journey, she tossed restlessly on her narrow camp bed. Suddenly, in the dead of night, she sat up, listening. A familiar voice seemed to be speaking. She slipped noiselessly to the canvas flap covering the entrance to the tent, and peeped out. There were two shadows out there, moving away in the moonlight. One, she recognized immediately; it as the Indian bank-clerk. Who was the other? They stopped, and half turned toward the tent. It was Huascar!

What was Huascar doing there at that time of night with that strange Indian? Why were they pointing at her tent? What did it all mean? The two shadows were walking again... Then the peace of the night was broken by a neigh, and the young girl saw a picketed horse stamping in the shadow beyond. Huascar vaulted into the saddle, while his companion loosed the picket-rope, still talking and occasionally nodding toward the tent. Then they both disappeared, and silence descended again on the sleeping camp.

Marie-Thérèse could not sleep all night. Huascar's unexpected reappearance was in no way calculated to calm the half-expressed terror which still haunted her, and which she refused to acknowledge, stifling what she called her cowardice. Had she anything to fear from Huascar? She could not believe it. She knew quite well that the Indian loved her, as a faithful dog does, she thought; and she felt certain that she could count on his devotion if she were in any danger.

And yet! And yet!... And yet what? What danger could there be? It was absurd! She was becoming as ridiculous as those two old ladies with their crazy legends! With that, she decided not to say a word to either Raymond or her father. She was not going to be taken for a child afraid of every shadow. But she would question Huayna Capac Runtu on the very first occasion.

This occasion presented itself during the first stage of the next day's journey. Marie-Thérèse, the Marquis, Raymond and old Monsieur Ozoux led the way. Uncle François, at first delighted with the prospect of a mule ride, soon determined to get off again. Riding along the edge of precipices, his mount felt ten times too high, and he was sure that he would be safer on foot and, at certain times, on all-fours. He gradually became convinced that his mule would slip, and determined to dismount, at a point where two riders could not pass abreast.

The whole cavalcade was thus stopped, while those behind called on the scientist to go ahead, and he vowed that he would do nothing of the kind, twisting in his saddle and trying to discover the best way to get off. Immediate action of the Indian bank-clerk saved the situation, and probably Uncle François' neck. Getting off his own mule, Runtu squeezed down the line, and catching Monsieur Ozoux's mount by the bridle, led it on to a broader path and safety. Raymond, the Marquis and Marie-Thérèse could not do less than thank him.

When they moved on, Marie-Thérèse and the Indian were riding side by side.

"Well, señor Huayna Capac Runtu?" she smiled at him.

"Oh, señorita, let us forget all those illustrious names, which died with my ancestors. The only one I have a right to now is that by which I am known at the bank—just plain Oviedo, like everybody else."

"Yes, I remember now. That is what you called yourself when you came to me from the bank. Well, señor Oviedo, can you tell me what you were doing outside my tent last night with Huascar, my former servant?"

Oviedo-Huayna Capac Runtu did not budge, but his mule swerved slightly. He reined it in.

"So you saw Huascar, señorita? An old friend of mine. He arrived late at night, on his way to Cajamarca, and knowing I was at the camp, halted here a minute to see me. I remember now, we did stop outside your tents. When I told him you were there, he asked me to keep watch over you... He went on immediately afterwards."

"Do I need somebody to keep watch over me, then? Am I in any danger?"

"The ordinary dangers of a journey like this. A mule may miss its footing, or a saddle may slip off. In either case, it spells death. That is what Huascar meant, and that is why I myself chose your mule and girthed it up this morning."

"You are too kind," said Marie-Thérèse drily.

At this moment, Uncle François drew level with them. He had recovered his equanimity with the wider path, and spoke casually of mountain dangers.

"All the same," he added, "I wonder how Pizarro managed to bring his little army through here."

Marie-Thérèse threw him a look which, had he seen it, would have toppled the clumsy scientist into a ravine, mule and all. But he remained serenely unconscious.

"It is extraordinary," acquiesced Oviedo. "I have made rather a study of it. At some points, the road was so steep that the horsemen had to dismount and almost drag their chargers after them. A single false step would have hurled them thousands of feet below. The defiles were then just practicable for the half-naked Indians, and think what it must have been for armored men, with the menace of an unknown enemy above them."

"But what were the Indians doing all this time?" asked Raymond, approaching in his turn.

"Nothing, señor. They were awaiting a visitor, not a foe. Messages had been exchanged which..."

"One question," put in the Marquis' voice. "Do you suppose that, if King Atahualpa had for one minute imagined his 50,000 men were incapable of defending him against a hundred and fifty Spaniards, that he would have behaved as he did? No, he merely felt contempt for their weakness. But he was wrong!"

"Yes, señor, he was wrong." The bank-clerk bent his head humbly over his saddle-bow. Then, straightening himself again, he pointed to a peak towering above. "He should have appeared in those defiles, like the horseman yonder, and all would have been finished. The Sun, our God would still be reigning over the Empire of the Incas!"

As he said these words, the clerk seemed to have grown to a giant. His sweeping gesture took in the whole huge mass of the Andes, making of it a pedestal for the Indian above them, sitting motionless on his horse, and watching their caravan.

"Huascar!" exclaimed Marie-Thérèse.

All recognized Huascar. From that moment, until they had left the first chain of the Andes behind them, that silhouette of horse and man dominated and haunted them—sometimes behind, sometimes before, but always above them: a promise of protection, or a menace?

CHAPTER II

After another night in camp, the travelers came in sight of the beautiful valley of Cajamarca, smiling below them in striking contrast to the somber mountains around. Thus did this happy valley appear to the astonished eyes of Pizarro's men. It was inhabited in the days of the Conquistador by a race far superior to those with which the Spaniards had met on the other side of the mountains, as was clearly shown by the taste of their clothes, the cleanliness and comfort of their homes. As far as the eye could reach was a prosperous plain, watered by a wide river, abundantly irrigated by canals and subterranean aqueducts, broken up by green hedges and well-cultivated fields; for the ground was rich, and the temperate climate favorable to farming. Immediately below the adventurers lay the little city of Cajamarca, its white houses twinkling in the sunlight, like a precious stone shining in the dark girdle of the Sierra.

About a league beyond, in the valley, Pizarro could see columns of steam rising to the sky, and showing the position of the famous hot baths of the princes of Peru.

There was also a spectacle far less pleasing to the Spaniards. The lower mountain slopes disappeared under a cloud of white tents, covering an area of several miles.

We were amazed, wrote one of the conquerors, *to find the Indians holding so proud a position, and this sight threw confusion, and even fear, into the staunchest hearts. But it was too late to turn, or to show the slightest weakness, and after carefully exploring the ground, we put on the best faces that we could, and prepared to enter Caxamarxa.*

Flowing over with such memories, and wild with excitement at finding himself in a land which he knew so well by hearsay, Uncle François stood up in his stirrups, and held forth interminably on the Cajamarca of his dreams. Instructed by Oviedo Runtu, he showed them the exact spot where Atahualpa and his 50,000 warriors had awaited Pizarro. Uncle François himself felt no fear of this huge army, massed in the hidden fastnesses of a continent discovered by Christopher Columbus just forty years before Pizarro's wild venture. He felt like a hero of antiquity, and was quite ready to give the order to charge.

There was nobody there to tell them, though, what were the feelings of the Peruvian monarch when he saw the warlike band of Christians, banners flying, corselets and morions gleaming, come out of the dark defile and advance into the rolling domains which, until then, no white man had ever seen.

Suddenly, Uncle François' mule bolted, and a burst of laughter went up from the whole party. Excited by the shouts and cries, the other mules followed their leader, helter-skelter down the incline. The obvious dénouement was not long in coming. Uncle François' mount, in a desperate effort to get away from the noise behind, rolled over, and the unfortunate scientist described a neat somersault. He was on his feet again almost at once, and soon set his anxious companions at rest.

"Thus it was," he laughed, "that Pizarro won his first battle."

Marie-Thérèse and Raymond appearing disposed to listen, he explained that, in the Conquistador's first fight with Incas, before he crossed the Andes, the little band of Spaniards, hard pressed, was saved by one hidalgo being unhorsed. The Incas, knowing nothing of horses or horsemanship, were so frightened by them that they fled, not daring to face this extraordinary animal which became two and still went on fighting.

Naturally, nobody believed him, though he was in no way drawing on his imagination. The whole story of the conquest of Peru is so extraordinary that one must forgive incredulity.

These facts, however, are vouched for by well-authenticated documents in the Royal Archives of Madrid, which Uncle François had taken care to study before starting for the Americas with his nephew. They were still laughing at his adventure and his story when their cavalcade reached the walls of Cajamarca.

It was nightfall as they entered the city. The first thing to attract their attention was the enormous number of Indians in the streets, and their silence. Cajamarca, with a normal population of between twelve and thirteen thousand, certainly sheltered twice as many souls that night. And still more people were coming.

On the highroad, the Marquis' party had successively passed file after file of Indians, plodding in the direction of their Sacred City. For Cajamarca may be called the necropolis of the Incas, and one can hardly take a step in its streets or avenues without meeting with some reminder of the splendor of a vanished empire.

It was easy to see, by the manner of the Quichuas crowding the historic roadways, that a religious pilgrimage had brought together this mass.

The amazement of the travelers, however, was as nothing to that of the inhabitants themselves, who had never before witnessed such an invasion. In the memory of living man, the Interaymi had never visibly moved the multitude in this manner. Even the great decennial fête had been rather the occasion for a general disappearance of Indians than for their appearance.

What did it all mean? The authorities were distinctly ill at ease, and the few troops massed at Cajamarca when the news came in of Garcia's Indian revolt at the other end of the country, had been put under arms. The doors of the city's eight churches were militarily guarded, for each one of these buildings might have made a fortress. The rest of the troops had been gathered in the main square, not far from the ruined palace in which stood the stone on which Atahualpa, last King of the Incas, was burned alive.

These ruins were the goal of the Indians' long pilgrimage over the mountains, the visit to that stone being the religious and outward pretext for this mute manifestation by a conquered race.

Don Christobal, amazed at what he saw, nervously remembered that the great Indian revolt of 1818 had been preceded by just such happenings. Were the Interaymi festivals which began next day really to be the signal for one of those revolts which the governments of Peru had long decided were no more to be feared?

As he was putting this question to himself, the Marquis caught sight of the post office, and immediately dismounted. Raymond and Marie-Thérèse exchanged a smile. They were at last to know the name of the facetious sender of the Golden Sun bracelet. They pulled up their mules, and waited with an indifferent air that was perhaps a little affected. Ten minutes later the Marquis came out.

"I have the name and address," he said in a puzzled voice.

"And what is it?" questioned Marie-Thérèse.

"Atahualpa," replied her father, mounting.

"So the jest continues," said Marie-Thérèse in a voice that had changed a little.

"Apparently so. The clerk who received the parcel says it was brought in by an Indian, who said his name really was Atahualpa. That, after all, is possible."

"Well, as you have the address, we might pay him a little call," suggested Raymond.

"Exactly what I was going to say."

And Don Christobal turned his mule. Uncle François brought up the rear, vigorously taking notes, with his book resting on the pommel of the saddle.

They crossed a rivulet racing towards an affluent of the upper Maranon, passed San Francisco, the first Christian church built in Peru, and, after the Marquis had asked his way several times, finally reached a square teeming with Indians.

On one side of this square still stood ancient palace walls. There had been the last home of the last Inca King. There he had lived in splendor, and there he died a martyr. There had been the home of Atahualpa, and there had the post office clerk directed Don Christobal de la Torre!

CHAPTER III

Taken in the swirl of the crowd, the little cavalcade was gradually headed toward the ruined palace, and forced through its huge gates almost before the Marquis' party knew what had happened.

They were now in a vast courtyard packed with Indians. Some of them, standing erect, showed the proud foreheads of chiefs, but the great majority were prostrate round a stone in the center—the stone of the martyrdom of Atahualpa.

On the far side of this stone, standing on a rude bench, was a man draped in a poncho of vivid red. He was speaking in Quichua, while the crowd listened in reverent silence.

As the party of strangers rode into the courtyard, a sharp voice behind them interrupted the psalm-like recitation of the man in the red poncho.

"Speak Spanish, and everybody will understand," it said.

The Marquis and Marie-Thérèse turned. Behind them was their bank-clerk traveling companion, bowing as if to make them understand that he had intervened to do them a favor. Extraordinarily enough, this interruption, almost sacrilegious as it was, did not stir a man. The Indian in the red poncho paused for a moment, and continued in Spanish.

"In those days," he said, "the Inca was all-powerful, and a vast army bowed to his will. The city was surrounded by a triple wall of stone, in the heart of which stood the citadel and the home of the Brides of the Sun. The Inca, knowing no fear, and ignorant of all treason, allowed the white men to enter the city and received them as friends, as envoys from that other great emperor beyond the seas.

"But the leader of the strangers, doubting the generous heart of the Inca, had divided his army into three bands, marching toward the city in battle array. Then the Inca said, 'Since they fear our hospitality, let us all leave the city, so that peace may enter their hearts.' Thus it was that, when the Conquistador rode through our streets, he met not a living soul, and heard no sound but the stamp of his own warriors' feet."

Here the speaker stopped, as if to gather his thoughts, and continued:

"This was at a late hour in the afternoon. The stranger then sent an ambassador to the Inca's camp. He sent his brother, Fernando, and twenty horsemen. The Inca received Fernando on his throne, his forehead adorned with the royal *borla*. He was surrounded by his officers and wives. The Stranger came with words of honey, and the Inca replied:

" 'Tell your leader that I am fasting until tomorrow. Then will I and my chiefs visit him. Until then, I allow him to occupy the public buildings on the square, but no others. I will decide tomorrow what is meet.'

"Now it happened that after these good words, a Spaniard, to thank the Inca, put his horse through its paces, for the king had never seen such an animal. And several of those present showed fear, but the Inca himself remained impassible and ordered them to be put to death, as was just. Then the ambassadors drank *chicha* in golden vases brought to them by the Brides of the Sun, and returned to Cajamarca.

"When they told their leader of what they had seen, the splendor of the Inca's camp, the number of his troops, despair entered the soldiers' hearts. At night, they saw the Inca's camp-fires lighting up the mountain-sides, and blazing in the darkness like a multitude of stars."

The Indian paused again, then went on:

"But the Stranger, intent on evil, went among his men, spreading the shameful words which gave them new courage. The next day, at noon, the Inca's body-guard advanced toward the city. The King could be seen above the multitude, carried on the shoulders of his princes. Behind him, the ranks of his own soldiers stretched as far as the eye could reach. The city was silent, save for the cry of the sentinels on the citadel walls, reporting the movements of the Inca's army.

"First, there entered into the city three hundred ser-vitors, chanting songs of triumph to the glory of the Inca. Then came warriors, guards, lords adorned with silver, copper, and gold. Our Atahualpa, Son of the Sun, was borne above all on a throne of massive gold. Now, when Atahualpa, with six thousand men, had reached the great square without seeing a single white man, he asked:

" 'Where are the strangers?'

"And a monk, whom none had seen until then, ap-proached the Inca, a cross in his hand. With the monk was an interpreter of our race. The Inca listened while the priest told him of his religion and urged him to aban-don the faith of his fathers for that of the Christian God. Atahualpa replied:

" 'Your God was put to death by the men to whom he gave life. But mine still lives in the Heavens, and shines upon his children.' "

At these words, the Indians surrounding the little band of Europeans turned toward the sun, just about to vanish behind the Andes, uttering a strange cry, a cry of mingled farewell and hope handed down by generations as the salutation of their faith to the God of Day. Above the reverently bowed throng, a purple sky awaited the coming of night.

The scene was so grandiose that Raymond and Marie-Thérèse could not restrain a movement of admiration. There could be no doubt of it: the Sun god still had his true worshipers, as in the tragic days of Atahualpa. To know it, one had only to look at this trembling mass of men, who had kept their language and their traditions through so many centuries. They had been vanquished, but not conquered. Perhaps it was true after all that back there in the mountains, in some city unknown to all but themselves, guarded by the rampart of the Andes and the eternal snows, there lived priests who passed their lives feeding the sacred fires.

After their salutation to the Sun, the Indians resumed their kneeling posture, many, strangely enough, making the sign of the cross as they bent to the ground. Where did that sign come from? Was it only another instance of the extraordinary mingling of cults and creeds so often seen, or did it go even further back? Some historians say that the conquerors found it already used by the Incas. Did some early Christian adventurers, then, found the twin empires of the Americas? While Uncle François dreamed on, lost in such conjectures, the priest in the red poncho, took up the broken thread of his narration:

"Pizarro and his men, armed for battle, were hiding in the halls of the vast palace surrounding the square. There the monk who had spoken to Atahualpa rejoined the Stranger, and said to him:

" 'Do you not see that we wrestle in vain with this dog's pride? His troops are coming up by the thousand. Strike while it is not too late!' "

The silence became, if possible, more intense. The man in red, about to tell of what he called the Crime of the Stranger, straightened himself on his pedestal until he dominated the whole assembly.

" '*Santiago!*' With that accursed battle-cry, Pizarro's men hurled themselves on the Inca and his guard. Horse and foot charged out of the palace in which they had been hidden, smashing in the Indian ranks. A terrible panic seized Atahut and his followers, who fled in all directions. Nobles and servants, princes and guards, fled before the terrible horsemen, who trampled down all before them.

"They made no resistance. They could not, for they were unarmed. Nor could they flee, for all the doors and streets were barred by the corpses of those trampled to death in a vain effort to escape. So terrible was the press, the whirling swords driving our people ever further back, that one wall of the square fell. Hundreds fled through this opening and scattered in all directions, the Spanish horse in pursuit.

"Atahualpa's throne, borne hither and thither in the crowd, was finally reached by the Spaniards. He would have been killed there and then had not Pizarro intervened. In doing so, he was wounded in the hand by one of his own men. The nobles carrying the royal litter were cut down, and the Inca was seized by Pizarro. A soldier named Estete tore the *borla* from his forehead, and the captured monarch was conducted to a hall nearby.

"With the capture of the Inca, all resistance ceased. The news spread through the country like wildfire, and all thought of real resistance was gone. Even the thousands of soldiers encamped round the city took fright, and scattered.

"The only being which might have kept the Indians united was prisoner of the strangers.

"That night, the Inca supped with Pizarro. He showed surprising courage, and remained impassible throughout the meal.

"The next day, the sack of the city began. Never had the Spaniards seen so much gold and silver. Atahualpa, quick to see their greed, offered Pizarro to buy his liberty by covering with gold the floor of the room in which they were. Finally, he declared that he would not only cover the floor, but also fill the room as high as he could reach.

"With that, he made a mark on the wall with his fingertip; and Pizarro, accepting, ordered a red line to be drawn round the room at that height. The room was seventeen feet by twenty-two long, and the line was drawn nine feet from the ground."

At this point, the red priest stopped and walked slowly to a ruined wall.

"Here," he said, pointing to a still faintly visible line, "was the mark of the ransom. Atahualpa, moreover, promised to fill a neighboring room with silver, and asked for two months in which to fulfill the task. His messengers, chosen among the Spaniards' prisoners, were dispatched into all the provinces of the Empire.

"Meanwhile, the Inca was closely watched, for his captivity meant not only Pizarro's security, but also fabulous riches for the Conquistadors. The room filled gradually, Indians arriving daily with golden goblets, platters, vases and bar gold to lay at the feet of their prisoned ruler. On some days, we are told, as much as 60,000 pesos of booty was brought in.

"To hasten the gathering of the ransom, Pizarro sent his brother Fernando to Cuzco, the greatest city of the

Incas. With them went a messenger from Atahualpa, at whose orders the priests stripped the Temple of the Sun, and the inhabitants gave up every scrap of precious metal in their possession. Fernando brought back with him, besides a mass of silver, 200 full loads of gold.

"Now faced with the problem of taking his plunder from the country, Pizarro ordered the melting-down of the hundreds of objects massed in the treasure-room. The finest pieces sent from temples and palaces were set aside for Charles V, to show the Emperor what a wonderful land had been added to his possession—all the rest was to be reduced to ingots.

"The native jewelers, obeying Atahualpa, worked night and day for a month to carry out this task. When the ingots were weighed, the Spaniards found that they had gold to the value of 1,326,539 pesos de oro. This would mean, in modern currency, and taking into consideration the altered value of money, more than three and a half million pounds sterling, or close on fifteen and a half million dollars.

"But now that the ransom had been paid, Atahualpa was still not set free. His captors accused him of fomenting a rebellion against Charles V, and threatened him with death. Atahualpa replied:

" 'Am I not a poor prisoner in your hands? Why should I do so, knowing that I should be the first to suffer if my people rose? And unless I give the order, none will raise a hand against you. Even the birds in my states hardly dare fly against my will.'

"But his protestations of innocence had little effect. Pizarro's men were convinced that a general uprising was being prepared. Patrols were doubled, and every man of the little army slept under arms.

"Pizarro did all he could, or pretended to do so, to save the Inca's life, but in vain. His followers demanded it, and Atahualpa, brought to trial, was found guilty and sentenced to be burned alive. On the 29th of August, 1533, his fate was proclaimed in the great square to the sound of bugles, and two hours after sunset, he was taken to the stake. Atahualpa left this hall in chains! He passed through this door on his way to martyrdom!"

Once again, the red priest left his rostrum, walking here and there through the crowd, evoking by deed as well as word the last hours of the last Inca. The silence was intense, and his voice, alternately grave and impassioned, rang out like a clarion note.

In the sad story, the Indian orator had omitted all that showed the immense courage of the Conquistadors and the cowardice of the Inca's followers. Everything was attributed to the treachery of the Spaniards.

"So Atahualpa died here, at the stake!"

Menacing and prophetic, the priest turned toward the spot where Christobal de la Torre and his companions, hemmed in by the crowd, had listened, as motionless as any of the faithful present.

"And I say unto you, cursed be all the sons of those who came to us with a lie in their hearts! They shall die like dogs, and never know the blessed palaces of the Sun. They shall die unblessed, the liars who say that Atahualpa abjured his faith! The Son of the Sun remained true to the God of Day!"

There was a threatening murmur in the crowd. Around the Sacred Stone, it grew to a roar. How dared those strangers come there at such a time? Centuries of slavery can never bend backs so low that they will not straighten at certain times. The descendant of Christobal de la Torre had met one of those hours.

CHAPTER IV

Men, women and children began to press toward the group of riders. Raymond, first to realize the change in the humor of the mob, spurred them.

"We must get out of here! Steady, and forward all!"

The Marquis, superbly cool, followed, as if reluctant to show his back to any horde of Indians. The menace in the voices grew clearer. He looked around, and drove his spurs home, until his mount reared and plunged into the crowd, clearing a space around it.

The mob was howling now, and knives were being drawn on all sides, when a giant Indian pushed his way toward the Spaniards. Marie-Thérèse, Don Christobal and Raymond recognized Huascar, before whom his countrymen made way with evident respect and dread.

"Back!" he shouted, taking the young girl's mule by the bridle. "Who touches the Bride of the Sun is a dead man!"

At these words, the crowd parted. Silence succeeded the tumult of a moment before.

"Let the strangers pass," ordered Huascar.

He himself escorted them to the ancient palace gates.

Outside, on the plaza, they met a police patrol. The sergeant, in undertaking to escort them to the inn, was eloquent on their imprudence in coming to a neighborhood peopled by fanatical Indians on the eve of the Interaymi.

The Marquis wished to thank Huascar, but the Indian had vanished. Marie-Thérèse and Raymond, both very pale, had not a word to say. Uncle François was also silent, and did not take a single note.

At the inn, they found only one vacant room, in which they all gathered. Raymond was the first to utter the thought which was worrying them all.

"Suppose it is true!"

"Yes, suppose it is true!" repeated Marie-Thérèse.

"What? Suppose what is true?" demanded the Marquis, refusing to understand.

"The Bride of the Sun!"

They were all silent for a moment, bent under the weight of one amazing, absurd, monstrous thought. And they exchanged anxious, frightened looks, like children who are being told some terrifying fairy tale. Raymond broke the spell:

"You heard what Huascar said. 'Who touches the Bride of the Sun is a dead man!' Those were his own words!"

"Just a manner of speech," said Uncle François, sounding unsure. "It cannot be anything else."

"Anything else? What do you mean?" demanded the Marquis violently.

"Well, it could not be... the other thing. If Marie-Thérèse was... was the Bride of the Sun, they would not have let her leave."

"Are we all going mad? After all, we are masters here!" burst out Don Christobal. "There are the police, and the troops. All those rascals out there are our slaves. Upon my soul, we are all raving!"

"Of course!" exclaimed Marie-Thérèse.

"All the same, I think we ought to get out of Cajamarca as soon as we can," said Raymond, going to the window and looking out.

Night had fallen, and with it silence. The square outside was deserted.

Suddenly there was a knock at the door, and a servant brought in a letter addressed to Marie-Thérèse. She tore it open and read aloud:

"*Return to Lima at once. Leave Cajamarca tonight.* It is not signed," she added, "but this warning comes from Huascar."

"And we should follow his advice," said Raymond.

There was another knock at the door. This time, it announced the arrival of the Chief of Police, who was anxious to know what had happened. He had heard of the incident at Atahualpa's palace, and had moreover been warned by an Indian, an employee at the Franco-Belgian bank at Lima, that it might be dangerous for the Marquis and his companions to show themselves in the streets on the following day.

It was obvious that the man feared trouble, and would have given anything to see the party a hundred miles away. When he learned that they were ready to leave at once, he busied himself about finding them fresh mules and a guide, and furthermore dispatched four troopers to escort them as far as the railway station.

They left Cajamarca at eleven o'clock that night, and the return journey was made at double the speed at which they had come. Raymond would let nobody rest, and forced the pace throughout.

It was not until the following night, safe in the train for Pascamayo, that they realized the ridicule that attached to their hasty flight.

"Just like a pack of children frightened out of their lives by Agnes' stories," said the Marquis.

Back in civilized life again, they were all surprised at their panic. After all, the whole thing could be so naturally explained—fanatics resenting the presence of strangers at a religious festival, and nothing more. The best thing they could do was to forget it as soon as possible. Uncle François restored the party's gaiety by going through the same performance which he had rehearsed on landing.

Forty-eight hours in Lima completely dispelled the cobwebs. Marie-Thérèse found a great deal of work awaiting her, and forgot her fears in a maze of figures which took her to Callao early, and kept her busy at the offices until late in the afternoon, when Raymond came to fetch her.

One afternoon, about eight days after the adventure at Cajamarca, the tap at her window which announced Raymond's arrival came earlier than usual. Marie-Thérèse got up, and threw open the shutters. Raymond was not there...

Then she retreated with a half-strangled scream. Was it possible? In the rapidly gathering darkness, she could not be sure, and leaned out of the window to see better... That thing, swaying in the darkness, looked just like the sugar-loaf skull... She retreated into the room, trembling in every limb, and turned around. From the dark corners of the chamber two other shadows, the suitcase and cap skulls, were advancing slowly, swaying as they came toward her...

For a moment, Marie-Thérèse thought she had lost her mind. Then she made a violent effort to regain control of herself. Dead skulls could not come to life. And yet, they were coming toward her, swaying horribly, above shadowy bodies!

A desperate scream for help was choked in her throat. "Raymond!" and nothing more.

The three living skulls had hurled themselves upon her, gagged her, and now, throwing the inanimate girl over their shoulders, hurried through the black hole of the open window. Marie-Thérèse's own car was waiting there, her servant at the wheel, smiling strangely.

Their mummy hands, horribly living, lifted the girl into the trunk, and the three monsters, like three larvae, climbed in after her.

Then the car shot down the street.

BOOK III: THE TRAIL OF THE PONCHOS

CHAPTER I

Meanwhile, Raymond, wandering through Callao until the time came to call for Marie-Thérèse, was strolling up the Calle de Lima. He had just come from the Darsena docks, where the harbor engineers had been giving him some bad news. In the present condition of the country, they said, any venture in the deserted gold mines of the Cuzco was hopeless.

The last two days had brought news of fighting from the other end of the country. Or, in any event, cartridges were being used up, even if there was no attendant damage. Everybody had thought Garcia was feasting at Arequipa, but the pretender had evaded his enemies and attacked the Republican forces between Sicuani and the Cuzco. It was even rumored that the city of Cuzco itself had fallen into his hands.

If this was true, the outlook for Raymond's business was bad. His company, thanks to the influence of the Marquis de la Torre, had obtained a concession from President Vointemilla, but it would not be worth the paper it was printed on if Garcia proved victorious. Superactive by nature, the young engineer could not endure the thought of long months of enforced idleness before him, at least until the revolution had been settled in one way or another.

As he came into the Calle de Lima, Raymond pulled out his watch. He found that he still had a few minutes to spare. Much as she loved him, Marie-Thérèse did not like being interrupted at her work, so he turned into the Circulo de los Amigos de las Artes for a drink. This establishment, though known as a club, was in reality a huge café and reading-room. The ground floor was packed with people discussing the latest events. Cuzco was in every mouth, and it was noticeable that even Vointemilla's warmest partisans now had a good word to say about Garcia.

A stampede of shock-headed newsboys, shouting the latest edition of an official paper, tore past the café, scattering still wet sheets and collecting coppers. One of the customers climbed onto a table and read out a proclamation by the President, urging calm and giving a categorical denial to the report of the capture of Cuzco. General Garcia and his troops, the President announced, were bottled up in Arequipa, all the sierra defiles were in the hands of Government troops, and the traitors would be hurled into the sea, or chased into the great sand deserts. The proclamation concluded with a reference to Indian troubles in the suburbs, attributing them to the usual Interaymi effervescence, and dismissing them as negligible. Cheers for the President ended the reading of his manifesto. Wavering allegiances were at once restored, and it was generally agreed that his statement was superb.

Raymond left the café a little happier, though he did not really place a great deal of faith in the official denial. Night had fallen and he walked briskly, now fearing that he might be late. As he went, he remembered his first day's walk through this same labyrinth of narrow streets. Then he caught sight of his fiancée's veranda in the distance, and noticed that the window was open, as on the first day.

There she had sat, the dedicated businesswoman, with her brass-covered green ledgers. What a brain she had! And to think that the pair of them had been such fools over that Golden Sun bracelet... Something to laugh about in future years!

"Marie-Thérèse!" he called.

There was no answer. He walked up to the window And called again:

"Marie-Thérèse!"

Still no answer. He peered into the room, trying to see where she might be hiding. But there was nobody there.

"Good God! Marie-Thérèse!"

Raymond walked into the room. There could be no doubt: that desk knocked down, those books on the floor, that curtain torn from its rings, this broken pane in the window told the story. Silence greeted his shout for help. Not a servant, not a soul in the place, and all the doors open!

"Marie-Thérèse! Marie-Thérèse!"

Hardly knowing what to do, Raymond ran into the deserted courtyard, and then back into the office. There could be no doubt: Huascar—that dog, whom she had trusted, and who claimed to love her—and his Indians had carried her off. Horror-stricken, furious, Raymond searched the room for some clue.

The scoundrels! He swore aloud as he pictured Marie-Thérèse struggling in Huascar's arms and calling for help in vain. That was where he should have been, instead of listening to all those fools in the café. He could have laid his hands on Huascar then! That was the man they should have been watching instead of being thrown off the scent by all those wild legends about the Bride of the Sun!

An Indian thirsting for revenge! Of course! He saw it all now, and remembered how Huascar had last left that same room, driven out by Marie-Thérèse. The insolent dog, with his fist raised in menace!

As idea after idea swept across his brain, Raymond stared helplessly at the blank walls around him. What could he do? He jumped back into the street and hesitated. No clue here—only the doors of closed stores and sightless walls—a pit of gloom.

Suddenly, he heard voices, and leaped into action. At the corner there, under a lantern, was a wine-shop, the only living thing in this dead street. He ran toward it, kicked the door open, and almost fell on top of Domingo, the night watchman.

"Where is your mistress?"

Domingo, taken aback, mumbled indistinctly. He thought that the señorita had returned to Lima as usual with the señor. Her car had gone by just a little while ago.

"Her car? Really?"

Domingo confirmed it. There were not so many cars in Callao and Lima.

"Who was driving?"

"Her usual driver."

"Libertad?"

"Si, señor, Libertad."

"Did he say anything to you as he went past?"

"No, señor, he did not see me."

"Did you see your mistress?"

"The top was up, señor, and it was traveling fast... No, señor!... That is the truth. I swear it!"

Raymond seized the man by the collar, and shook him like a rat.

"What were you doing here? Why were you not with your mistress, at your post?"

"I meant no harm, señor. A Quichua offered me a drink here... Real *pisco*, señor..."

Raymond, without listening, dragged the protesting man through the streets and into the empty office. When he realized what had happened, Domingo would have torn his hair out with grief, but Raymond, seizing him by the throat, drove him to the wall and looked into his eyes. A fool or a traitor, which was he?

Told to speak, and speak quickly, Domingo answered Raymond's volley of questions without a minute's hesitation. The señorita could not have been carried off without the aid of Libertad, a rascally half-breed to whom the señorita had given work out of pity. The day and hour had been chosen by someone who knew the place well, for on Saturday afternoons, there were no workmen or clerks on the premises.

"When you went out to drink, was the car already waiting?"

"Yes, señor. It had been for there half an hour."

"Was the top up?"

"No, señor. Libertad was sitting in it alone."

Releasing his grip, Raymond dashed into the street again and started running toward the main avenue. If Marie-Thérèse had been carried off in her own car, it would be easy to trace her part of the way. As Domingo had said, there were not so many cars about.

As he dashed around the corner, Raymond came into sharp collision with a man emerging from a doorway, who swore vigorously. Raymond recognized him at once, and gave such a shout that the chief of police—for it was he—fell into a defensive posture.

"Forgive me, señor... I am Raymond Ozoux... the fiancé of Señorita de la Torre... She has been carried off by Indians!"

"Doña Marie-Thérèse? That is not possible!"

In a few words, Raymond told the little gentleman what had happened. He found ready sympathy and belief.

"I was on my way to dine with a friend just opposite. A minute while I tell them that I cannot come, and I am with you."

The Chief hurried across the street while Raymond, with an indignant snort, moved on toward the harbor, questioning shopkeepers and pedestrians as he went. So far as he could gather, the car had about half-an-hour's start of them. He was convinced that he had seen the last of the Chief of Police, but he had done the little man an injustice, for he had hardly gone two hundred yards before he heard footsteps behind him.

"You did not wait, señor? Well, here I am. Natividad is always to be relied upon."

Though his real name was Perez, the Chief of Police was known throughout the city as Natividad, a nickname earned him by his cherubic face, and of which he was rather proud.

Raymond found the little man prejudiced enough against the Indians, even for his taste. Natividad hated the Quichuas, and believed them capable of anything.

Just before they reached the harbor, at the corner of the narrow Calle de San Lorenzo, Natividad seized Raymond by the arm and drew him to the wall. The street was deserted, and lit only by feeble rays from a low glass-paned door a few steps ahead. This door had just been opened, and a man peered out cautiously.

Raymond stifled a desire to shout. He had recognized Huascar!

The Indian whistled, and two shadows, wearing wide-brimmed Indian sombreros, detached themselves from the wall at the other end of the street. They rejoined Huascar, who had closed the door behind him, and exchanged a few rapid words. Then the two walked off in the direction of the harbor, and Huascar disappeared as he had come.

Natividad, pressed against the wall, held Raymond's hand in a grip that imposed silence.

"What is it? What does it mean? Perhaps she is in there," the young man whispered.

Gesturing to the engineer to stop talking, Natividad crept toward the door, and, at the risk of being discovered, peeped through the uncurtained panes. Raymond, looking over his shoulder, saw a room full of Indians sitting at tables, but neither smoking nor drinking. Huascar was walking up and down between the tables, in deep thought. Then he vanished up a staircase leading to some room on the first floor.

Natividad had apparently seen enough, for he dragged Raymond into the shadow of a neighboring porch.

"I cannot make it out," he said. "What are they all doing here during the Interaymi? I thought every Quichua in the city had left for the mountains. There should not be one here for the next ten days. But I cannot believe Huascar has anything to do with the kidnapping. He wouldn't tell his secret to all the Indians of Peru, when he knows that nearly every one of them can be bought for a few centavos!"

"Wait before you make up your mind. We can at all events find the car. I am sure Huascar knows where Marie-Thérèse is. We must not lose sight of him."

"We shall not have to wait long," replied Natividad, stiffening at a fresh noise from the other end of the calle. "Here are those Indians coming back with horses. What does it mean? Madre de Dios! Is it possible? The Interaymi!... Silence!"

The clatter of hooves on the cobbled roadway showed that quite a strong cavalcade was approaching, and the watchers drew back farther to the shelter of an alley nearly opposite the low door, from which they could still see all that was happening around it.

As the cavalcade rode up, the door opened again, showing all the Indians standing up, and apparently waiting for somebody.

Huascar appeared first; after him, an Indian whom Raymond recognized at once for the Red Preacher of Cajamarca; lastly, a man in a lounge-suit of impeccable cut—Oviedo-Huayna Runtu himself. Then an incredible thing happened. All these men who had remained motionless before Huascar and the priest bent on their knees, humbled their heads to the ground before the bank clerk.

The troop of horses and mules had halted before the low door, and men with lanterns came out of the house. The bank clerk was the first to vault into the saddle, Huascar holding his stirrup. Then Huascar and the Cajamarca priest mounted, ranging themselves on each side of the leader, but just behind him.

Huascar turned in his saddle and made a sign. Every Indian in the party threw open his poncho, showing beneath it, in the light of the lanterns, another cloak of brilliant red.

91

"The Red Ponchos!" gasped Natividad, grasping Raymond's arm.

There was a whistle at the end of the street, answered by another a long way off, at the other end of the Darsena quay, and the cavalcade started.

Raymond made as if to follow, but Natividad held him back.

"Wait, and listen! We must know which way they are going!"

CHAPTER II

Hunched forward, he listened, then turned to his companion.

"The Chorillos road. Unless I am much mistaken, they are following the car."

"Come on; we must get after them! Where can we get horses?"

"Follow me. We can do better than that. We have the telephone and the railway." And once again he took up his litany: "The Red Ponchos! The Red Ponchos!"

"What do you mean by that? Red or gray, it's all one. Those men belong to Huascar's band, and helped him. That seems pretty clear to me."

"Quite right, quite right. I agree with you now, young señor," replied Natividad, puffing by Raymond's side as they hurried toward the railway station. "Yes, indeed. They are all in it... The Red Ponchos... The Priests of the Sun..."

Raymond stopped dead. Natividad's last words at last made him understand. He remembered, in a flash, all the legends told by Aunt Agnes and old Irene. And they had seen fit to laugh.

"Good God!" he groaned, and began running again. As he ran, he shouted to his companion: "But we'll catch them yet, and you'll arrest them all!"

"I shall do what I can. But there are at least thirty of them, and there are not enough troops in Callao to send a squadron in pursuit. Every soldier the city could spare has been sent into the sierra against Garcia."

"You can telephone Lima."

"And they'll take me for a madman, as they did ten years ago," replied Natividad enigmatically.

"Will we get to Chorillos before them?"

"Yes, there's a train in ten minutes' time."

"It seems to me we would have done better to follow on horseback. Then we could have found out where they were going. Thirty of them, are there? Only damned Indians, though. I wouldn't mind tackling the lot myself."

"This way is the best..." And Natividad added in an undertone: "They wouldn't believe me ten years ago. Well, it's starting all over again."

Raymond, intent on reaching the railway station, did not hear him. He could only think of those mysterious Indians on the highroad out there.

"We shall lose their trail," he groaned.

"You need not fear that," replied the Chief of Police. "Their road runs alongside the railway line. If we see a car waiting on it, we stop the train. If we overhaul the Red Ponchos alone, we go on to Chorillos, and wait for them there. I'll see that the police expect them. Nothing is lost yet, Señor Ozoux."

At the railway station, Natividad found he had just time to telephone his instructions to the Chorillos police. No car coming from the direction of Callao was to be allowed to pass.

They were talking to the guard of the express when a Lima train steamed into the station, and they saw the Marquis, Uncle François and little Christobal appear.

"Where is Marie-Thérèse?" shouted the Marquis as he caught sight of Raymond, and ran toward him. "Why are you alone? Where is she? What has happened? Speak, boy!"

Little Christobal, clinging to Raymond's legs, reiterated his father's questions, while Uncle François' long shanks took him wandering aimlessly round the little group. The guard blew his whistle, and Natividad pushed them all into a carriage just as the train started.

"Yes, she has been carried off by the Indians, but we know where she is. She is at Chorillos." Raymond's attempt to reduce the force of the blow to the Marquis partly succeeded.

Then he explained what he knew while Don Christobal, raging in his corner, swore to kill with his own hands every Quichua in the country. Little Christobal, understanding only that his sister was lost, sobbed bitterly. But what had given the others the alarm?

The Marquis explained that Aunt Agnes and Irene, going to church for the evening angelus, found that the Golden Sun bracelet had been stolen from the shrine of the Virgin of San Domingo. They had returned home in a panic, to find the Marquis nearly distracted with fear. Going to his club for the first time in a week, he had there found an anonymous letter warning him to watch over his daughter day and night throughout the Interaymi. This letter, a twin of the one received at Cajamarca, had been waiting some days. It particularly warned him not to allow his daughter to go to Callao on Saturday.

It was then seven o'clock, and going home to find that neither Marie-Thérèse nor Raymond were back, he had at once rushed to Callao. Little Christobal, refusing to listen to orders, had followed his father and Uncle François.

Raymond listened like a man demented. He was silent, but his mind was in a turmoil. To think of such a thing! In a country where people used telephones and traveled by rail! It was too horrible, too incredible, yet horribly credible. There was no doubt in his mind now as to the reasons for the abduction.

Natividad, closely questioned by the Marquis, finished by telling all he knew, and left them little hope. While loath to cause pain, he could not disguise certain facts. In a sense, too, he was triumphant. A conscientious official, he had once almost ruined his administrative career by reporting on certain Quichua customs, dealing notably with the ritual murder of women and children. He had been laughed at, and called a lunatic— now the Red Ponchos were at work again!

The silence of despair greeted his words. Then, anxious to reassure them, the little gentleman insisted that the Indians could not go far with their precious burden. All the defiles of the sierra were held by Vointemilla's troops. They would always give assistance to the police, and the Indians were bound to run into them as soon as they left the Costa. The chief thing was not to lose the trail.

They had now reached the point where the railway line joined the highroad running parallel to the sea, and all eyes were fixed on the great white band stretching out there in the moonlight. At first, it was bordered by a few tumble-down cabins and bamboo cottages, but soon there was only the nakedness of a huge sandy plain before them. Raymond, the Marquis and Natividad, grouped at the windows, searched the night, while Uncle François took little Christobal in his arms and strove to console him. But the boy insisted on being held up, that he also might see out, moaning the while:

"Marie-Thérèse, Marie-Thérèse! Why have they taken my big sister? Marie-Thérèse!"

Suddenly, the same cry broke from them all:

"The car!"

There it was, standing before the gates of a lonely hacienda. Natividad almost tore out the emergency cord, and the train, with a grinding of brakes, slowed down and then stopped. They tumbled to the line, Natividad shouting to the guard to go on, and send back police, troops and horses as soon as they could.

Raymond raced across the plain, while Natividad, panting in the rear, called out to him to be careful, and not to give the alarm. The young engineer drew a revolver as he reached the motor, ready to shoot down the first man he saw. But there was nobody there. The car was empty, and the courtyard of the hacienda was deserted, peopled only by the blue shadows of moonlight.

The gates were wide open, and he entered cautiously. Some of the buildings around the courtyard were in ruins; all were manifestly deserted. On his right, the *bodega*, or store-house; on his left, the proprietor's *casa*. Here again, the doors were open.

Raymond returned to the car, and there was rejoined by the Marquis and Natividad just as he lit one of the headlights. There was not a sound to be heard, and they followed the young man in silence. As they entered the first room of the house, a heavy, pungent perfume greeted their nostrils.

Raymond, leading the way, took a few cautious steps, and then fell back with a cry of horror. The furniture of the place was scattered in all directions, and there was blood everywhere.

"Marie-Thérèse!"

The Marquis and Raymond, both calling out at the same time, were as suddenly silent again. Both seemed to have heard a faint voice answering them.

"It's up there!" shouted the young man, dashing toward a staircase leading to the first floor.

All could now distinctly hear a low, prolonged moan. Raymond, slipping on the stairs in his hurry, rose again with a white face. His hands were red with blood!

CHAPTER III

The first two rooms were empty, but bore unmistakable signs of a desperate flight and struggle. Then a landing, a door and a dark cupboard, from which a loud cry for help now resounded throughout the deserted hacienda. Raymond, gesturing to the Marquis to turn the light into the corner, bent down, and dragged a body from the cupboard.

It was Libertad!

Covered with knife-wounds, the little servant was on the point of' death, struggling for air. They took him into the next room, and threw open the windows, while Raymond questioned him brutally.

"Where is your mistress?"

A feeble hand pointed toward the sierra, and Raymond stood away from the dying man. That was all he wanted to know. The Red Ponchos were already on the road to the mountains with his fiancée.

He dashed down into the road to find Uncle François with little Christobal. The boy, climbing into the car, had discovered his sister's cloak there, and was crying over it. He threw himself into Raymond's arms, but was roughly pushed aside while the young engineer raged impotently.

What could he do? Anything for a horse, a mule, something to carry on the pursuit! The irony of it! That car there, which had served for the crime, was useless now on the narrow rocky mountain pathway which they must follow.

Then little Christobal, listening with wide-open eyes, started. He had heard a noise at the far end of the courtyard. Could there be horses in that deserted *bode-ga*? It sounded just like hooves stamping on a plank flooring. Then the child heard a faint neigh.

Raymond had vanished, and Christobal, running toward the farm buildings, slipped through a half-open door. Yes, there was something there... llamas... three llamas... but thin, miserable creatures, worn out by the heavy loads of years, and incapable of carrying even a child. But llamas do not neigh.

The boy slipped round the corner of the building, and stopped short in the shadow. Sitting motionless a few yards away was a horseman, watching the house. At his stirrup, attentively immobile as the horseman, was a llama—one of those light, fine-limbed, long-necked beasts which carry a man's belongings and follow him like a dog.

As Christobal caught sight of them, the horse shied. The rider reined it in, and swore, but his oath was cut short by a shot. A shadow had risen in the night, only a few feet away, and had fired; the rider rolled from his saddle, while the shadow, seizing the horse's bridle, swung itself into his place.

Little Christobal ran toward it.

"Tell your father I've bagged one of them," shouted Raymond, turning his mount and riding for the sierra.

The child, without answering, ran after the llama, which in its turn was following the horse. His little fingers caught in its wool, he checked it with the words one uses to llamas, scrambled up and dashed after Raymond. Uncle François, on the roadway, was passed by two black streaks, and left alone there, speechless.

Meanwhile, in the room on the first floor, Libertad was making his confession. Natividad had realized, and had made the Marquis realize, the great value to them which this might have. Nor, to tell the truth, did he forget the value of the Marquis as a witness to this confession, which he regarded in the light of a valuable piece of fresh evidence in his case against the Indians generally. For this twofold reason, Natividad was merciless, and forced the little servant to speak till his last breath.

This confession, made in gasps and groans, built up by questions and answers, and cut short by death, showed clearly that the abduction had been long planned, and that the daughter of the Marquis de la Torre had been chosen as the victim of the Interaymi at least two months before the festival. That was as clear as the wonderful tropical night outside.

Two months before, Libertad had first been sounded, and he had not long resisted the temptation of the money offered him. All he was asked to do was to drive the car to a certain spot on a certain day, without looking to see what was happening behind him. For this, he was to receive two hundred silver *soles*, of which fifty were paid to him in advance.

"And who did you make the bargain with?" demanded Natividad.

"With a clerk from the Franco-Belgian bank who sometimes came to see the señorita. His name is Oviedo."

Don Christobal started. Oviedo-Huayna Runtu, the intruder of the Cajamarca trip! If he had planned to kidnap Marie-Thérèse at Callao, that voyage must have been particularly disagreeable to him. That would explain his close watch over them, and perhaps also the hint to the police at Cajamarca, which resulted in their hasty return to Lima.

"When did you first know the date chosen?" questioned Natividad, holding up the man, who was choking.

"This morning. Oviedo came to see me. He told me that a man would say to me, *Dios anki tiourata* [good-day], and that I was to obey that man. I was to take the wheel, not turn my head, and drive where I was told to go."

Libertad's story, told in jerky sentences, showed that he did not really know until the evening what had been plotted. Though he did not move or look, the sound of the struggle at the open window told him what was happening. It was then too late to draw back, and, when the order came, he drove the car to the calle San Lorenzo, where they stopped for a minute before a low door. Huascar came out, exchanged a few words with the occupants of the car, and ordered him to take the Chorillos road, and not to stop until he had reached Ondegarda's hacienda. There was not a sound behind him throughout the journey.

At the hacienda, when his passengers got out, he had instinctively glanced sideways, and had seen the señorita, unconscious, being lifted out by three dwarves with horribly-shaped heads. They took her into the *casa*, while he, more dead than alive, waited where he was, anxious only to be paid and to get away.

Then they were overtaken by a troop of mounted Indians, all wearing red ponchos, and led by Oviedo. Huascar was also with them, and ordered Libertad to come into the house. To his surprise, he found there half a dozen women, veiled in black, and guarding the door to another room.

"The mammaconas," gasped Natividad. "We can have no doubts now... Speak, Libertad... Speak, and God may forgive you."

"Yes, the mammaconas," said the lad, feverishly. "But I did not know! God will forgive me... The señorita, too, will forgive me... You must save her... She was so good to me... And I betrayed her... betrayed her for two hundred silver *soles*... They did not know I understood their language... They said that Atahualpa would have a beautiful bride... And they fell on their faces before her when she passed..."

"You saw her, then?" demanded the Marquis, bending low over the prostrate figure at his feet to catch the faint words.

"Yes, I saw her... She was so good... And I sold her for two hundred silver *soles*..."

"Tell us what happened next," interrupted Natividad. "Was she no longer unconscious?"

"She came out of the room, held up by women in black veils... The three dwarves were dancing around her... She seemed to be in a dream... They have terrible poisons and perfumes... My sweet señorita... wrapped in a gold veil... her face was hidden... only her eyes, staring sightlessly before her... The mammaconas were all around her... and the dwarfs were dancing. I saw it all, because they had left me alone, and I looked out of the window... they put her on a mule... in front of one of the mammaconas... and the others followed... Yes, señor, it is true... all these stories you hear in the ranchos... Quite true... the dwarves followed her, señor... Oviedo was there... they had prepared everything in this hacienda... I believe they murdered the owner and all his people...

"Yes, I saw it all... I did not care then that I had not been paid... I watched... And the Red Ponchos carried off my mistress... they are taking her to the Temple of the Sun... It is the Interaymi... But you will find them first... You must... And God will forgive me."

Libertad closed his eyes and fell back, but seemed to recover his forces with the last flicker of life, and opened them again.

"What happened to you?" asked Natividad. "Was it in trying to save your mistress?"

Libertad smiled bitterly, and tried to cross himself, but his arm fell nerveless by his side.

"Huascar," he said. "He came into the room, and when I asked him to pay me, pointed to the two hundred silver *soles*... they were on the table there... I thought it was not much for betraying my mistress... I did not know that was what they wanted... When I told him so, he asked me what I would have done if I had known... I answered I would have asked double the amount..."

"What then?"

"Then he drew a knife and came at me... I ran, but he followed... He stabbed me once, and I escaped, but he followed... I ran upstairs... He stabbed me again and again... When I fell, he thought I was dead... and I am... I am... dying... oh!... Lord, have mercy!"

Libertad's last moment had come. The Marquis and Natividad, bending over him, were startled by a shot coming from outside, and rushed downstairs.

They found Uncle François by the car, staring down the road. When they asked him where Raymond and little Christobal were, he gazed back as if not understanding, and vaguely answered that he was looking for them.

Don Christobal and Natividad, turning to look in the direction the old scientist was staring, suddenly saw two shadows dash across a moonlit stretch of road and vanish in the darkness of a ravine leading into the mountains, and spanned above by the railway bridge. Raymond on his horse, little Christobal on his llama, did not even check for an instant at their hail.

Hardly had the hooves beats died out in the depths of the ravine than the sound of galloping horses came from the right, on the Chorillos road.

A moment later, a band of riders appeared.

CHAPTER IV

"Horses!" exclaimed Natividad. "Then we have them. They are probably making for the Cuzco, or someplace around Lake Titicaca, But they are bound to pass through Vointemilla's lines, and we shall catch them at Canete or Pisco."

As Natividad had surmised, the riders were cavalrymen sent out from Chorillos at his order. They ran toward them. Uncle François was questioning the Marquis, who did not answer. Indeed, Don Christobal, doubly anxious now that his son had left his side, could not contain himself. Hardly had the troopers dismounted than he swung himself into the nearest saddle, and rode off after Raymond.

"Sheer madness," growled Natividad. "If they ever catch up with the Indians, they are doomed."

"What are we going to do now?" demanded Uncle François.

Marie-Thérèse's fate moved him deeply, particularly from a literary point of view, but under the circumstances, he asked no better than to be kept a little in the background.

"We can only follow at a distance," replied Natividad.

"Excellent... excellent... find out where they are making for, and all that sort of thing."

"There are still laws, a police force and troops in Peru, señor. We are not afraid of the Indians."

After saying this, the Chief of Police turned to the four soldiers who had joined them, and who represented

106

what remained of the military force on the Costa. Uncle François, already delighted with Natividad's plan of following at a distance, approved of it even more warmly when he found that this little escort was to accompany them.

Three policemen mounted on mules, coming from the direction of Callao, now appeared on the road. Natividad at once requisitioned the mules for his expedition. Before starting, however, he went back into the *casa* to write a hurried letter to President Vointemilla, explaining what had happened. He did so with a certain malice, remembering that ten years ago, this same president had been Chief of Police, and had threatened to suspend him for his "crazy reports."

One of the policemen, entrusted with the letter, started back toward Callao at once. The two others were ordered to take charge of the hacienda and begin a preliminary inquiry. Then Natividad and Uncle François mounted two of the commandeered mules, the third being taken by the soldier whose horse had been carried off by Don Christobal. When the soldiers saw that they were heading for the sierra instead of Chorillos, there was a grumble, but Natividad silenced them.

"Forward!" he ordered, and they, in their turn, entered the ravine.

"We can, at all events, travel as fast as the mammaconas," said the Chief of Police to Uncle François.

"The mammaconas? Were they here then?"

The scientist, intensely interested, urged his mount alongside Natividad's.

"Yes señor... the mammaconas... and three priests from the temple... Only they may touch the Bride of the Sun, señor... For the past fifteen years. I have known all this, but they called me a lunatic. Why should we suppose that the Indians have changed? Do they not eat, drink, and get married just as they did five centuries ago? If their outward customs have not changed, why should their secret rites have done so? Why, señor, why? But nobody believed me. It all began when I was a young man. I had to investigate a mysterious crime, the only possible explanation for which was a religious one. You must not forget that you are dealing with Incas to this day... And I got my knuckles rapped!

"Five years later, when the Orellana girl disappeared, they treated me in the same fashion. So I let them give whatever explanation they liked, and worked on my own. I speak Quichua like a native now, señor. I also learned Aimara, which is their sacred language in the Cuzco and around Titicaca... That's where they are making for now; some hidden temple, where their priests have been worshipping the Sun since the days of the conquest."

Uncle François looked at his companion suspiciously. Were they all engaged in a huge practical joke at his expense? This Chief of Police was singularly calm under the circumstances, off-handed, almost joyful.

"We are sure to catch them, are we not?" he asked.

"Certainly, señor. *Dios mio*, be content! We will catch them... How can they possibly escape? We are on their heels. If they stick to the mountains, they run into our troops; if they go down into the Costa, every *corregidor* is at my beck and call."

There was a moment's silence, and he went on:

"Take that cloak from your saddle-bow and put it on, señor. The nights are chilly, and we are nearing the *cordilleras*... It's the only road, you see. They must have passed here. At dawn, we shall be able to see their trail distinctly... If only those crazy people who dashed on ahead do not make fools of themselves... A plucky youngster, little Christobal... We shall soon overhaul them... One does not climb these mountains as a bull jumps over the barrier at the ring..."

Natividad's garrulous flow of words was interrupted by a chuckle from Uncle François. Not a little astonished, he asked him what he meant, but Monsieur Ozoux contented himself with replying:

"I understand, I understand."

Natividad, who did not understand, eyed him doubtfully.

Just before daybreak they reached the first masses of the Andes. Their mounts did not appear over-tired, and, after a two-hours' halt at a wayside *guebrada*, where beasts and men obtained food, they continued the journey. Over them towered the giant mountain chain, blazing in the molten light of dawn.

The half-breeds at the *guebrada* could not, or would not, give them any information as to those they followed. That the Indian cavalcade had not stopped there, however, was certain, or larder and loft would have been empty. Natividad, convinced he would get nothing else out of the men, forced them, in the name of "the supreme government" to exchange two strong mules for two of the horses.

Shortly after they had started again, they came on unmistakable traces of a strong party of horse. Thistles, and the great yellow flower of the amancaes, trampled flat, showed where hooves had passed.

"We are closing on them now, señor," said Natividad.

Uncle François, coughing knowingly, assented in such a detached manner that Natividad began to have serious doubts as to the mental state of that illustrious scientist.

Before long, though, he was worrying a great deal more about something else. So far, there had not been a sign anywhere of the Indians' first pursuers. Uncle François, on the other hand, was thoroughly happy, and seemed to be enjoying the scenery.

As they climbed steadily upwards, the road was becoming more and more dangerous, twisting and turning around the mountain-side. Peaks, sky, and precipices; in the blue of the distance, a few mountain goats, all four feet joined together, balancing on some rocky point.

The cold was now intense, and the soldiers grumbled openly. When Natividad reminded them that they were serving "the supreme government," they let it be inferred that they did not give a tinker's damn for the *supremo gobesnie*, but nevertheless followed.

"Are you sure of those men of yours?" asked Uncle François.

"As sure as of myself," replied Natividad, determined to be optimistic.

"What are they? Indians?"

"Quichuas, of course... Where else would we get soldiers?"

"They do not seem to me to be enthusiastic militarists."

"A grave error, señor. They are delighted to be soldiers. What else could they be?"

"They are volunteers, then?" questioned the scientist. And to Natividad's stupefaction, he produced his notebook.

"No, not volunteers, illustrious señor... We send troops into the Indian villages, and arrest every able-bodied man who has not bolted. Then we enroll them as volunteers."

"Charming! And you are not afraid that they may turn on you after you have armed them?"

"Not in the least. After the first few days, they decide they are so much better off under the colors that they would not go back to their families for anything... You should see them join in the recruiting afterwards! They make very good soldiers... These men are only annoyed at being taken into the mountains; they would die for Vointemilla."

"So much the better," concluded Uncle François philosophically. And he added, to Natividad's growing amazement: "But why insist on their coming with us? We can find those other Indians just as well without their aid."

Natividad jumped. What kind of a man was this? Then his attention was suddenly drawn to the road again.

"There! Over there! They camped there."

At this point, the mountain path widened to a kind of little plateau, on which were unmistakable traces of a recently-pitched camp. The ashes of the fire had not yet been swept away by the wind, and remains of food littered one corner. Natividad, convinced that he had found the first resting-place of the escort of the Bride of the Sun, urged on his party.

"It is strange," he said, "that we should have seen nothing yet of the Marquis, little Christobal, or your nephew."

"Why worry? We'll find them all, sooner or later."

"What?"

"Sooner or later—someday... Hello, what's the matter? This beast of mine won't move. Hi-yo."

Calm and collected, quite different from the frightened Monsieur Ozoux of the flight from Cajamarca, he urged on his mount, but the mule refused to answer to his heel. Then Natividad, pressing forward to see what was the matter, saw the body of a llama stretched across the narrow path. Dismounting, he lifted its head, examined the nostrils, and then pushed the body over the edge of the ravine.

"Little Christobal's llama," he pronounced. "The animal has been ridden to death... Poor child! I wonder where he is."

Uncle François, busy with his notebook, refused to get excited.

"With my nephew, probably. Even if Raymond had left him behind, his father must have come upon him."

"That is possible, of course," said Natividad, doubtfully.

"Is this llama-riding common over here?" questioned the scientist, intent on acquiring knowledge.

"No. Children sometimes amuse themselves with it if the llama is willing. Rich people give them to their sons occasionally. Christobal probably had his."

"I would never have believed a llama capable of going so far, and so fast."

"No pack llama could. But that was a good one, trained to carry light weights and travel fast. Probably used to being ridden by children... I wonder where they found it... Your nephew's horse, too... in the hacienda stables, I suppose... A tragedy might have been avoided had they not."

The little party rode on. A little later, taking a sharp corner, they came suddenly upon Raymond and the Marquis, the former on foot, and the latter mounted. But Little Christobal was not there.

CHAPTER V

Raymond was pale, but the Marquis was livid. So they appeared to Natividad; as to Uncle François, he had not his glasses on, and he noticed nothing disquieting in their appearance.

"Those scoundrels have both my children now," groaned Don Christobal in answer to Natividad's eager questions, and told what had happened.

Badly mounted for mountain roads, the Marquis had found great difficulty in following the kidnappers. Several times he had been on the point of abandoning his horse, but, thinking it might be valuable later on, had kept to it. Once or twice, he had been obliged to dismount and drag the unwilling beast behind him.

At dawn, he reached the Indians' camp, which he searched in vain for some personal sign of his daughter. She was evidently too well guarded. Finally, he found the llama's body, but being convinced that Raymond was with little Christobal, had not worried overmuch. Then, a little further on, he found Raymond, but alone.

Raymond, powerless to interfere, had seen little Christobal carried off by the same Indians who already held Marie-Thérèse. When they started on their wild ride, as soon as the road became steeper, the llama had rapidly outpaced Raymond's horse. Little Christobal, riding it hard, would not stop, and soon vanished ahead.

Two hours later, Raymond had lost his horse in a ravine, throwing himself from the saddle only just in time, and narrowly saving his own life by clinging to a projecting rock. He continued his pursuit on foot, and finally came in sight of the boy, just as the llama, exhausted, burst a blood-vessel and fell. He had called to little Christobal, but the boy, unheeding, had run on, crying, "Marie-Thérèse! Marie-Thérèse!"

They were right on the Indians then, and Raymond could see them far above him on the zig-zagging mountain-path. They had checked their horses, waiting for the boy to catch up to them. Then, one of the Red Ponchos bent down, lifted him up to his saddle-bow, and hurried on with his new captive. Raymond was too far away to open fire, and the Indians had at once spurred on, soon leaving him far behind. The Marquis had come up a short time after.

"You must not despair, Don Christobal," urged Natividad. "Your news is not all bad. They are only just ahead, and cannot escape us. They must pass through Huancavelica, and there, we have troops to help us."

Natividad ordered one of the soldiers to dismount and give his mule to Raymond. The man was indignant, and continued protesting in a weird jargon as he trotted afoot behind the cavalcade. In this manner they reached a point where the road forked, one branch going on up into the hills, the other stretching down toward the coast. They had all turned up the former when the dismounted soldier turned—he would go no further, but would descend to the coast; and once there, he would report to his superiors the manner in which he had been treated by a mere civilian. Natividad wished him an ironical good-bye, and he started, but only to reappear a moment later, waving a soft felt hat in his hand.

"That belongs to Christobal!" exclaimed the Marquis.

They turned their mounts, grateful for the lucky sign which had saved them from a grievous mistake. Natividad alone hesitated, wondering whether this was not an Indian ruse. They advanced slowly therefore, until the mud and sand on the banks of a torrent just below showed beyond doubt that a large number of mounted men had passed that way and restored Natividad's serene belief in the ultimate success of their search.

"So they're doubling back to the Costa. They must have been warned that the passes were guarded... All they have gained by the detour is avoiding Chorillos... Perhaps they are making for Canete... Well, they must stop somewhere, and then we'll have them!"

After an hour's rest, they hurried on again at top speed, one of the soldiers giving his dismounted comrade a lift behind.

"Did you, then, ever think that we might not catch them?" asked Uncle François of Natividad, with an enigmatical smile.

"Why not, señor? Between you and me, it is about time we did catch them... I, for one, shall not feel happy if señorita de la Torre and the boy are still in their hands on the last day of the Interaymi."

"Do you mean that the boy is in danger?"

"Speak lower, señor, speak lower... Nothing is too young, too beautiful, or too innocent for the Sun. Do you understand?"

"More or less. More or less."

"You people do not know what horrors they are capable of... They still have their priests... You might blink at facts if it were only the ordinary Red Ponchos, but there are also those three monsters... You always find them together in the old burial-grounds... When one dies, the other two are put to death... Or when a king died, they sacrificed themselves on his tomb... They still exist, those monsters, those high-priests of the sacred slaughters... They still exist, señor."

"Do they?"

"You, señor, are a savant, and know about the Temple of Death. But do you know how many dead were found buried with the mummy of Huayna Capac? Four thousand, señor! Four thousand human lives sacrificed to honor the dead—some by suicide, others strangled, knifed or suffocated... And the House of the Serpent... But I prefer not to tell you what happened there..."

"Tell me some other day... You make an admirable guide. When we return, I will tell the President how grateful I am to his government for having made the most erudite of police officers my cicerone."

"I beg your pardon, señor?"

Natividad, completely taken aback, could only stare at his interlocutor.

"Nothing, nothing! I am only joking!"

Scandalized at such levity, Natividad turned away with an indignant snort, while Uncle François chuckled. That worthy gentleman had now quite made up his mind that there was a plot afoot against him, and sternly refused to be "taken in." The joke was rather tiring physically, but he would not cry for mercy. As to all these hair-raising stories, he would take them for what they were worth. Let them play their pranks until they tired of them.

The more he thought of it, the more he became convinced of the truth of his deductions. His antiquarian's eye rested lovingly on the traces of that long-dead Inca civilization which they met. Here, aqueducts that would have made the Romans wonder; there, remains of the great road which ran from end to end of South America. They were all dead, those Incas. Yet these people wished to make him believe that those vanished warriors

116

and priests had carried off a boy and girl of today to offer them as a sacrifice to equally forgotten gods!

They had now left the arid ranges and dusty wind behind them, and reached a little village nestling in green fields at the foot of the mountain. A babbling stream, tumbling down from the *Cordilleras*, had transformed this corner into an oasis of verdure, in which Uncle François would willingly have passed a few hours. But now that they were in flat country again, Raymond, the Marquis and Natividad increased the pace feverishly. Uncle François, still determined not to show that he had fathomed their plot, was careful not to protest.

Once or twice, they stopped to ask questions, but it was difficult to obtain information. Hamlets were rare, and the Interaymi festivals had drawn away nearly the whole population. The few Indians they met received their questions with evident suspicion, and even hostility. Nor would money loosen their tongues.

Fortunately, there were half-breeds more ready to talk, and they learned that Huascar and his companions were riding hard. Nobody had seen Red Ponchos; presumably the priests had concealed the ceremonial raiment imposed by their ritual for the reception of the Bride of the Sun. They were traveling so fast that nobody had had time to notice whether they had a captive boy or young woman with them. At the questions on this score all their informants began to grow uneasy, and turned away with evasive sentences.

Huascar and his men had about two hours' start, but it soon became evident that they were gaining ground steadily. Natividad could not fathom the meaning of the Indians sudden turn toward the sea, this riding into a town where, normally, everything must be against them if the alarm was given.

They reached Canete at nightfall, Raymond still leading. There was a big fête on, with torchlight processions and the deafening noise of fireworks set off by delirious roisterers. Half the native population was under the influence of drink, and Natividad, trained to understand the populace, at once saw that the town was in a state of dangerous effervescence.

Of all the towns in Peru, Canete is perhaps the one which shows most markedly that strange admixture of the new and old. Factory chimneys tower to the sky side by side with Inca aqueducts which to this day bring the water of the Rio Canete to the surrounding plantations. Just above the town are still the remains of the huge native fortress demolished some two hundred years ago by the then viceroy of Mañdelova when he needed materials for the defenses of Callao.

Natividad's first visit was to the *corregidor*, who told him that the town was celebrating Garcia's victories. It was now certain that the rebels had captured Cuzco, and routed the Federal forces. Natividad then told him of the plight of the Marquis de la Torre's children. The Mayor was skeptical, and showed it. Indians committing such a crime, he said, would never have dared pass through a town.

"They could not stop in the Sierra," said Natividad, "and had to make for somewhere. Perhaps they intend taking boat, and reaching Arequipa by sea. They could get up into the Cuzco that way."

"That is more than possible," replied the *corregidor*, anxious to rid himself of the troublesome visitor. "A troop of strange Indians has, in fact, passed through the town. They bought provisions, and then hurried on to

Pisco. They might have a boat ready there... Personally, I can do nothing for you. I haven't a single soldier or policeman to dispose of. They have all gone to fight Garcia."

At this moment, an extraordinary procession passed under the corregidor's windows. A dancing, singing procession, at the head of which Natividad recognized his four troopers. He opened the window and shouted menaces, but they passed unheeding.

In a sad mood, Natividad rejoined his companions. Without any explanation, he told them they must follow to Pisco, and they started again. Natividad, in a dark mood, would answer no questions.

Don Christobal, hearing that the Indians were making for Pisco, grew hopeful. He was known in the town, having a branch of his business there, with big guano warehouses in the harbor, and a considerable coolie station on the Chincha Islands, which are just off the town. There he could speak with authority, and make the *corregidor* listen.

They reached Pisco dog-tired, on mounts that could hardly stand. Uncle François alone displayed a calm and unconcern which would have convinced the others he was mad, had they had time to notice him. The news of Garcia's victory had just reached Pisco, and the mob was even more delirious than that of Canete.

The Marquis, taking the leadership, led the way to his warehouses, only to find them completely deserted. There was not a single employee there to answer his questions.

"To the *corregidor*'s, then," he ordered.

The four travelers had entered the main and only street of the town, and were riding toward the sandy central square when a thundering *feu de joie* made them pull up. The Indians were burning the sacred maize-leaf in honor of Garcia, to the grave danger of the little blue-and-white houses around. The inhabitants of these, well-to-do half-breeds, had locked themselves in, or taken to flight.

The madness of alcohol and the madness of fire crackers had taken firm hold of all that was visible of the population. The mob had pillaged a *pisco* distillery, and was enjoying itself thoroughly with that virulent spirit, which is made from a kind of Malaga grape, and takes its name from the town.

Natividad, casting round for a guide, found a half-breed sadly huddled under a doorway. He doubtless was one of those who had something to lose by the rioting; a house to be burned, or a cellar to be plundered.

"Follow me," he said, when asked where the corregidor could be found.

He led them along a plank pavement which was just beginning to burn, until they reached the corner of the arena, opposite the church. Four skinny palms adorned the center of the square, and at the foot of one of these a mob was dancing round a fire. Above, something was hanging from a branch. The half-breed pointed to that thing.

"There is the *corregidor*," he said.

Natividad, Raymond and the Marquis stopped short, mute with horror. The half-breed whispered a few rapid words to Natividad, who turned to run.

"Come on! Come on!" he almost screamed.

"Why this hurry?" demanded Uncle François, phlegmatically.

"Why? Why? Because they are going to eat him!"

"Not really?" drawled the scientist with mediocre interest. "Right away?"

But Natividad did not notice his tone. He was really running away, for he had not forgotten a scene in Lima, when the Guttierg brothers were torn from the presidency they had usurped by the same mob which had placed them there. Massacred, then hung over the cathedral gates; they were finally roasted and devoured by the populace.

So fast did Natividad flee, that Raymond and the Marquis could hardly keep up with him. Uncle François, bringing up the rear, was muttering to himself:

"Damn nonsense, damn nonsense... They're not going to frighten me."

BOOK IV: THE DICTATOR

CHAPTER I

Arequipa was *en fête*; the entire population of the city and its *campina* was packed in the main square and the adjacent streets to witness the triumphal return of the victor of the Cuzco—brave General Garcia, who had already been christened "the good Dictator," and who had promised his partisans that, within a fortnight, he would sweep out of the country President Vointemilla, the two Chambers, and the whole parliamentary system which, he declared, had ruined Peru.

This was language the Arequipinos loved and understood. Politics had always flourished in that part of the country, and all revolutions began there. And the turbulent inhabitants of Arequipa felt that it was a terribly long time since they had had a "savior" to cheer.

Now they had one; a particularly picturesque one, who was to appear on horseback. So they had all donned their Sunday clothes, and the women had flowers in their hair and more flowers in their arms to scatter before the hero. The Indian population, having sold its hens and vegetables in the market-place, joined the throng.

The square, for the occasion, seemed to have straightened out its tumble-down arcades, badly shaken by the last earthquake. The illusion was aided by brilliant-hued carpets, flags, banners and festoons which blazed in all directions and gave new life to the dilapidated walls. The cracked old towers of the church, the carved wooden balconies, flower-adorned galleries, and decorated windows were black with people. Above the city rose the Misti, one of the world's highest volcanoes, wearing a fresh cap, glistening with the snows of the night.

Bells chimed and cannons roared out. Then came silence, broken again by the sound of bugles and the roar of a thousand voices. The procession of the troops had begun. Contrary to European custom, it commenced with all the *impedimenta* of the camp. It was like a rout: Indians leading mules loaded down with baggage, provisions, and kitchen utensils; then a regiment of women bent under the weight of knapsacks, babies, and sacks of food.

The crowd cheered everything wildly, from the llamas loaded with captured Federal arms to the women, the *rabonas*, as they are called out there. These *rabonas* are a precious institution from the point of view of the Peruvian soldier; each man has his own, and she carries his baggage, buys all his food, and prepares his meals.

Then came the troops, Garcia, leading. Mounted on a splendid horse, wearing a brilliant uniform, he appeared like a star of the first magnitude in the constellation of his staff. A tall man, he showed head and shoulders above the generals and colonels prancing around him. His tri-color plumes waved splendidly in the wind, and the deafening rant of bugles accompanied him. Handsome, radiant, happy was he, nonchalantly curling his black mustache and smiling on all with brilliant white teeth.

Garcia smiled to the ladies as he passed under their balconies, and the ladies, showering down rose-leaves over horse and rider, called him by his Christian name, Pedro. In this triumphal fashion, he slowly rode round the square twice, and then came to a halt in the middle of it, between two guns, his staff behind him and, before him, two Indians bearing a standard, a quaint patch-work quilt of a flag, which was the token of submission of all the tribes to the new government. These men wore hats covered with variegated plumes, and had over their shoulders surplice-like tunics.

Five hundred infantrymen and two hundred horse had formed round the square. Young girls, clad in floating tunics and wearing Garcia's colors, advanced toward the general, their hands heavy with floral crowns. One of them made a little speech, while Garcia continued curling his mustache and showing his teeth. The speech over, he gallantly bent down and took all the crowns, passing them over his arm. Then he lifted a hand to command silence.

"Long live Liberty!" he shouted.

A hurricane of cheers arose. Again he lifted up the crown-charged arm, and again there was silence. He told them the program of the new Government meant "Liberty for all, except for evil-doers! With such a program, is there any need for parliaments?"

"No! No! No!" roared the crowd deliriously. "Long live Garcia! Death to Vointemilla! *Muera! Muera! Muera el ladron de saltier!* (Death to the saltpeter thief!)"—for Vointemilla was popularly supposed to have largely profited by some recent concessions.

Garcia was an orator, and, wishing to show it once again, told in a few words the history of the campaign that had ended in the rout of the "saltpeter thieves" on the Cuzco plains. To be seen and heard by all, he stood erect in his stirrups.

Then an incredible thing happened. The powers above actually dared spoil this splendid *fête*. It began to rain! There was a general rush for shelter in the crowd. Even the infantrymen lining the square broke their ranks, while the cavalrymen dismounted, took off their saddles and loaded them on their heads in guise of umbrellas. As to those soldierly ladies, the *rabonas*, they calmly threw their bell-shaped petticoats over their heads.

Garcia alone did not move. Furious at this spoiling of his triumph, he threatened his officers with immediate death if they dared leave his side. He did not even fall back into his saddle, but stood erect there, his crown-charged arm menacing the heavens. Then the Chief of Staff approached the Dictator, saluted thrice, and said:

"Excellency, it is not the fault of the sky. The sky would not have dared! The roar of your guns compelled the clouds, Excellency."

"You are right," replied Garcia. "And since the guns did the harm, let them repair it."

With which, a battery was rolled out into the square, and opened fire on the clouds. They thundered on until the short tropical storm had passed. Then Garcia, triumphant, shouted:

"I have had the last word with the heavens!"

The review was over.

CHAPTER II

Watching the proceedings from a window at the Jockey Club Hotel were the Marquis de la Torre and Natividad, both wild with impatience, for their only hope now lay in Garcia.

At Pisco, they had ended by discovering that the Bride of the Sun's escort had embarked in the very steam-tug used to tow the Marquis' own barges from the Chincha Islands to Callao. This once again proved that the Indians'scheme had been well thought out and prepared long in advance.

Securing a boat in their turn, the pursuers followed to Mollendo. There they took the train, and reached Arequipa only a few hours after the Red Ponchos—Uncle François still supernaturally calm, and Natividad beginning to despair of everything.

Chance favored them when they landed in this city of mad people, who would not even trouble to answer questions. Raymond recognized Huascar strolling through the streets, and tracked him to the house where Marie-Thérèse and her brother were kept prisoners. This was a low adobe building on the edge of the suburbs, and quite close to the Rio de Chili. It was openly guarded by a dozen armed Indians in red ponchos. Raymond and the Marquis soon found, however, that they could not even get as near as that line of guards. Fifty yards away from the house, Civil Guards stopped them, and ordered them back. Garcia's own troops were guarding the Bride of the Sun!

"Of course, Garcia cannot know," said the Marquis. "I know him, and though he has faults, he is not a savage. He once wanted to marry Marie-Thérèse. Let us go and find him."

But Raymond refused to lose sight of the adobe house. Had they listened to him, they would have forced their way to it at once. It was only after long arguing that Natividad convinced him such a step would be absurd. Lives are cheap during revolutions, and two or three corpses more or less in the Rio de Chili would not make it overflow its banks. Nor would they contribute greatly to the freeing of Marie-Thérèse and little Christobal.

He promised to be reasonable, but would not go with them when they returned to the inn for a meal; instead, he took up his post in a boat on the river, and thence watched his fiancée's prison and the armed men walking up and down before.

The Marquis and Natividad therefore, witnessed Garcia's triumph alone. Uncle François had been lost, or rather, had been left alone in the middle of the street, staring up at the Misti. He was now doubtless in the crowd somewhere, taking notes.

Garcia in all his glory was a sight which did not please the Marquis.

"I never thought he was that kind of man," he commented.

"Drunk with success," replied Natividad drily.

After the review, they followed the Dictator and his staff only to find their way barred by troops at the road leading down to the headquarters. Here the Marquis ordered the men out of the way with such insolence, and spoke with such assurance of "his friend Garcia," that he was allowed to pass, Natividad clinging to his sleeve.

The subaltern in command at the guard-room took the Marquis' card, and a moment later they were ushered upstairs. There were soldiers everywhere, some of them fast asleep on the staircase, their guns between their knees, so that the visitors had to pick their way upstairs over prostrate bodies.

Finally, their guide pushed open a door and ushered them into a bedroom, where Garcia was presiding over a meeting of the Cabinet he had appointed the previous day. Some of these high functionaries were seated on the Dictator's bed, others on the table, and one on a bundle of soiled linen.

They were received more than courteously. Garcia, who was in his shirt-sleeves, and still shaving, ran toward the Marquis with both hands outstretched, scattering white flakes from his shaving-brush as he came.

"Forgive me, señor," he said. "Antique simplicity! Antique simplicity! I receive you as I would a friend... for I trust you come as a friend, as a friend of the new Government. Let me introduce you..."

He began with the Minister of War, who was astride the bolster, and finished up with the Minister of Posts and Telegraphs, a hideous half-breed chewing cocoa-nut leaves.

"No fuss, you see," babbled on Garcia. "Antique simplicity. Cato, and all that sort of thing... Nothing like antiquity, señor, to make men... The good padres taught us that, and I took the lesson to heart." He laughed. "All that show is for outside... The crowds like it, and one must amuse the crowd! Did you see my review? Splendid, wasn't it? Magnificent soldiers... And the rain... Did you see what I did? Effective, eh?"

During all this verbiage, Garcia was thinking hard, and watching the new-omers' faces. He was far from being a fool. Were they, or were they not, ambassadors from Vointemilla? Would he accept a compromise, if they came to offer it? In a moment, his mind was made up; he would refuse, and risk everything on the result of this uprising, his large fortune and his life included.

At last, the Marquis was able to speak.

"I have come to ask the assistance of the master of Peru."

At these words the Dictator, who was washing the soap from his face, looked up in surprise over his towel. He knew that the Marquis was a personal friend of Vointemilla. Natividad looked away uneasily, for he was compromising himself horribly.

"The master of Peru," repeated the Marquis, "whose motto is 'Liberty for all.' I want him to restore to me my two children, who have been stolen."

"Stolen! What do you mean, señor? Those who have done this thing shall be punished. I swear it by my ancestor, Pedro de la Vega, who gave his life for the True Faith, and was killed by the infidels in the year of our Lord 1537 at the Battle of Xauxa, in which he received seventeen wounds while fighting at the side of the illustrious Christobal de la Torre!"

The Marquis had always said that Garcia was in no way descended from Pedro de la Vega, and Garcia knew it.

"Those same infidels have now carried off my daughter, Excellency."

"The beautiful señorita! But what do you mean by infidels? What infidels?"

"She has been kidnapped from Callao by the Quichuas as a sacrifice to their gods during the Interaymi."

"Sacrifice!... Interaymi!... But that cannot be, señor."

"I am sure of what I say, Excellency, and she has certainly been carried off. Let me introduce señor Perez, the Chief Inspector of the police of Callao. Like myself, he is devoted to your cause. He will tell you the same thing. Speak, Natividad."

Horrified at the form of the Marquis' introduction, Natividad stammered a corroboration. If Garcia did not win now, all that was left for him to do was to cross the Bolivian frontier.

The change in Garcia's manner was immediate. He did not want trouble with the Quichuas, his partisans and allies.

"But I can do nothing for you, señor. All this happened in Callao. Vointemilla is still master there, and you must go to him."

"They are now in this very city, imprisoned in a house which is guarded by your own troops."

"That is not possible. I should have known it. But if by some extraordinary fact this is so, you have not done wrong in coming to me."

"I knew I would not appeal to you in vain. As long as I live, I shall not forget this service. I have friends in Lima, señor! And this gentleman too," he pointed to Natividad. "The police of Callao is yours... Only accompany us to the gates of the city, and set my children free, and my life and my fortune are yours."

"I am afraid I cannot come myself, for I am expecting the British Consul. But I will send my Minister of War with you. You will find him just as useful." Garcia turned and whistled for the dignitary in question, who seemed in no hurry to move. "Go and see what is happening," he ordered, "and let me know... I believe you are in error, gentlemen, but I will do what I can for you."

Don Christobal and Natividad went out, followed by the Minister, whose enormous spurs made the hall and staircase echo.

Garcia closed the door.

"I wonder what it all means," he mused aloud, evidently much put out. "Ten to one, Oviedo Runtu is behind it. If he really has carried off the señorita de la Torre, the outlook for us at Lima is bad."

The door opened, and an officer announced the British Consul. This official was a big tradesman of the town, who had secured the commissariat contracts to Garcia's army by promising him the support of Great Britain.

Garcia began to speak of his soldiers, and the consul put in that the worth of an army resided more in the general who commanded it than in the men themselves. His compliment provoked a self-satisfied bow from Garcia, but he made the mistake of trying to improve it, and added:

"For, between you and me, Excellency, those troops of yours are not worth much, and if you had not been there to..."

"Not worth much! What the devil do you mean! Do you know what kind of fighting they have been doing in the mountains? Not worth much, indeed! Did you see a single laggard..."

"No, but the guard are all sound asleep now."

"Asleep!" Garcia swore, and ran to the door.

CHAPTER III

Garcia opened the door, and looked down the staircase, where he both heard and saw his guards sleeping. Pale with anger, the Dictator woke them, and ordered the officer to muster his men on the landing.

"My soldiers never sleep!" he declared to the consul. "Look at them. Do they look as if they wanted sleep. Come, my lads, a little exercise to keep you fit. Out of that window with you all!"

His outstretched arm pointed to the bedroom window, nearly five yards above the ground. The poor hussars looked at him, hesitated, and jumped. Remained only the officer.

"Well, and what are you waiting for, major? You should be with your men."

Then, as the officer did not move, he seized him around the waist, and threw him out of the window. The watching ministers and the consul, anxious not to take the same route, laughed heartily at the jest, and went to look into the courtyard. Those of the soldiers who had landed more or less safely were picking up three comrades with broken legs. The officer was being carried off, his skull fractured.

Just as this interlude ended, the Minister of War returned, still followed by the Marquis and Natividad.

"Well?" asked Garcia, closing the window.

"The Red Ponchos," replied the Minister, looking meaningfully at his illustrious chief. "Oviedo Runtu quartered them there, and added a few soldiers to the guard. They leave tomorrow night for the Cuzco."

"What else?" Garcia was nervously twisting his mustache.

"They know nothing of the young lady and the little boy."

"Excellency," burst in the Marquis, who could contain himself no longer, "you must have that house searched. I know they are in it. You cannot allow those scoundrels to go free! Your name would be tarnished forever if you did such a thing! It would make you the accomplice of murderers! On you depend the life of my son, the only heir of a great name which in the past has always fought for civilization, side by side with yours, and of my daughter, whom you once loved."

The latter consideration might have had little effect on the Dictator, who did not believe in confusing love and politics, but the sentence before, appealing to his sentiments as the representative of "a great name" moved him powerfully. He turned briskly to his Minister of War.

"But you must have seen something. I presume you searched the house?"

"If I forced that house, Excellency, every one of our Quichua soldiers would rise. Runtu has only to make a sign, and they cut all our throats. That house is sacred, for the Red Ponchos and the mammaconas are escorting the holy relics from Cajamarca to the Cuzco for the Interaymi fêtes. It is impossible, Excellency."

One look from the Dictator drove all his ministers from the room. When the door had closed on the last one, he turned to the Marquis.

"If your children are in that house, señor, it is terrible, but I can do nothing for you."

Don Christobal staggered under the blow, and leaned against the wall.

"Listen, Garcia," he said in a strangled voice, "if this horrible crime is allowed, I shall make you personally responsible for it before the civilized world."

He reeled, almost on the point of fainting. Garcia ran to his side, and held him up, but Don Christobal seemed to regain his forces at once.

"Hands off, you general of murderers!" he shouted.

Garcia went white, while the Marquis walked toward the door, turning his back on the Dictator though he expected to be stabbed at any moment. But Garcia controlled himself, and his lisping voice checked Don Christobal in surprise.

"Do not go yet, señor. I can do nothing for you, but I can at all events give you some advice."

Don Christobal turned, but ignored the hand which waved to a chair, and waited. He had already wasted too much time here.

"Speak, señor," he said; "time passes."

"Have you any money?" asked Garcia briskly.

"Money? What for? To..." He was on the point of saying "to bribe you," but stopped at a suppliant look from Natividad, who was gesturing desperately to him from behind the Dictator's back.

Garcia, remembering there was somebody else in the room, took Natividad by the arm, and put him out of the room without a word. Then he sat down at a little table loaded with papers, rested his head in his hands, and began to speak in an undertone, without looking at the Marquis, still standing and suspicious.

"I can do nothing for you against the Red Ponchos and the mammaconas. Their house, or their temporary quarters, must be sacred, for they have the relics of Atahualpa with them. You say your children are in that house as well. That may be, but I am helpless to prove or

134

disprove it. It is horrible, I agree, but I am powerless. You say that my soldiers are guarding the house? That is not true. I am nobody in all this. Who put them there? Oviedo Runtu. They are Oviedo Runtu's soldiers."

He paused for a moment.

"Who is Oviedo Runtu? A bank clerk with whom you may have had dealings in Lima? Yes, and no. He is a bank clerk, yes, but he is also the master of every Quichua in the country. He dresses like a European, and earns a humble living among us, yes, but meanwhile he is studying all our institutions, our financial methods, all our secrets. He earns two hundred *soles* a month behind a counter, but he is also perhaps a king. I don't know.

"King or not, all the Quichua and Aimara chiefs are his slaves. Huascar, your former servant, is his right hand man... If you ask me, he is a man who has dreamed of the regeneration of his kind! That's what he is. When I was preparing this revolt at Arequipa, Huascar came and offered me Oviedo Runtu's aid, and I accepted the alliance because I could not do otherwise. Do you understand now? It is not I, but Oviedo Runtu, who leads behind the scenes... He is in your way, as he is in mine... And, believe me, I am as sorry for you as for I am for myself."

"That's the man we seel. I can see his hand in it all."

"As I said before, force is out of the question. But though I cannot fight the Red Ponchos, *you* can bribe them. They are Quichuas, and any Indian can be bought. That is why I asked if you had any money."

"No, I have none," replied the Marquis, who had been listening to the Dictator eagerly. "We left in a hurry, and I had not time to think of it."

"Fortunately, though, I have."

Garcia whistled in a certain manner, and the Minister of Finance came in.

"Where is the war chest?"

"Under the bed, Excellency."

The Minister went down on his knees, and dragged an iron-bound box to Garcia's side.

"You may go now," the Dictator said.

When they were alone again, Garcia took a little key from his pocket, opened the box, and took out a bundle of banknotes, which he threw on the table. Locking the box, he pushed it under the bed again, picked up the notes, and handed them to the Marquis.

"Count them afterwards, and pay me back in Lima, when I am President. There is enough there to bleach every Red Poncho in existence. They are gentlemen who know the value of those little pieces of paper. Oviedo Runtu himself probably taught them. Good bye, señor, and good luck."

"Excellency," said the Marquis, forgetting that a moment before he had called this man a murderer, "I do not thank you... but if I succeed..."

"Yes, yes, I know... your life and fortune are mine."

"One word more. I shall try to bribe your troopers with the rest."

"By all means! By all means!"

"And if we fail, Excellency, I warn you that weak as we are, desperate as the venture may be, we shall attack those priests and their escort. Can we count on your neutrality?"

"Most certainly. And if by chance you kill Oviedo, I shall not have you hauled up before a court-martial!"

They shook hands, and the Marquis ran out. As he crossed the threshold, Garcia shrugged his shoulders.

"His daughter is lost, but he, the fool, has been bought by me. Ha! All this would not have happened if she had married me."

At the bottom of the staircase, the Marquis found Natividad waiting anxiously. In the street, they met Raymond, who had come to look for them. He was pale and agitated, and it was evident that some extraordinary event had made him leave his post.

"What has happened?" asked the Marquis.

"Back to the inn, quick! We must decide on some course of action. What did Garcia say?"

"That he could do nothing for us. But he gave me money and a piece of advice that may save them. But what made you leave your post? Are they still there?"

"Yes. Only one person has left the house, Huascar. I followed, determined to corner him, and kill him like a dog, if need be. He went straight to our inn, and asked for you. They told him you had gone out, but were returning. He then said he would wait, so I came to fetch you."

"They are saved!" exclaimed Don Christobal. "Why else should Huascar come to see me?"

"I don't like the man, and don't believe in him. You must not forget that we're dealing with a fanatic, and one who owes Marie-Thérèse a grudge."

"My wife found him starving in the street, and gave him shelter. I cannot believe he has altogether forgotten that. I have always thought he was in the whole business against his will, and determined to save Marie-Thérèse sooner or later. Hurry!"

"I hope you're right, but I don't believe it," replied Raymond. "We'll have him cornered in a minute, and if he doesn't answer my questions, he'll be sorry."

"You must not forget, Raymond, that they have hostages."

"Hostages which they will massacre even if we let Huascar go free! I would give anything to wring his neck!"

"And I, boy, would give anything to save my children."

The Marquis' tone was so icy that Raymond refrained from further comment.

Just before they reached the inn, Natividad noticed on the opposite pavement a tall old man leaning on a shepherd's crook, watching the door through which Huascar had entered. A ragged cloak hung over his thin shoulders, and a straggling white beard framed a face so pale that it was deathlike. Natividad stopped, and looked at him hard.

"I know that face," he muttered. "Who is it? Who is it?"

Don Christobal, entering the inn, told Raymond that he was going to their room, and asked him to bring Huascar there. The stairs leading up to the first floor were just inside the archway, and the Marquis, putting his foot on the first step, noticed Natividad staring across the road. His eye followed, and he also was struck by a sudden vague memory.

"Who on earth is that?" he wondered. "I have seen that man before…"

CHAPTER IV

Hardly had the Marquis entered the room than Huascar made his appearance, followed by Raymond and Natividad, like a prisoner with his two guards. The Indian swept off his hat, with a grave

"*Dios anki tiourata,*"

To wish a white man good day thus, in the sacred Aimara language, was a sign of great respect. Then, seeing that the Marquis did not respond to the greeting, Huascar began to speak in Spanish.

"Señor, I bring you news of the señorita and your son. If the God of the Christians, whom the benefactress worshiped, aids me, they will both be restored to you."

Don Christobal, though seething within, forced himself to the same calm as the Indian.

"Why have you and yours committed this crime?" he questioned, crossing his arms.

"Why did you and yours commit the crime of not watching over them? Had you not been warned? Huascar, for your sake, twice betrayed his brethren, his god, and his country. He remembered that the mother of the señorita once befriended a naked child in Callao. That is why he has sworn to save her daughter from the terrible honor of entering the Enchanted Realm of the Sun."

Don Christobal half held out his hand, but the Indian did not take it, smiling sadly.

"*Gracias*, señor."

"And my son, Huascar?"

"Your son is in no danger. Huascar watches over him."

"You say you watch over them! But tomorrow I may have neither son nor daughter."

"Neither son nor daughter will you have if you do not obey Huascar." The man's tone had become somber and menacing. "But if you obey, I swear by the head of Atahualpa, who awaits your daughter should I betray her, I swear by my eternal soul, that the señorita will be saved!"

"What must we do?"

"Nothing. You must abstain from all action. Do not pursue the Red Ponchos and put them on their guard. I will do everything if you and yours promise not to come near that house again. They know you, and when you appear, the mammaconas form the black chain around the Bride of the Sun. If a stranger appeared, they would offer her up to Atahualpa dead, rather than see her escape. Be warned, and do not leave this inn. If you promise me that, I swear that I will bring your son here, unharmed, at midnight. For your daughter, you must wait."

Don Christobal took down a little crucifix from a nail over the bed, and came toward Huascar.

"The señora brought you up in our holy faith," he said. "Swear upon this that you will do as you say."

Huascar held out his hand and took the oath.

"I have sworn," he said proudly, "but for me, your word is enough."

"You have it," replied Don Christobal. "We await you here at midnight. Gentlemen," he added, as Huascar's steps rang on the staircase without, "I have given my word, and you must help me keep it. I believe in Huascar."

"So do I," added Natividad.

Raymond was silent. He had been watching the Indian, and was unconvinced.

140

"What do you think, Raymond?"

"I don't like it. Perhaps I am mistaken, though. I feel that Huascar hates me, and I do not love him particularly. We are not in a position to judge one another. Midnight will show."

Natividad, going to the window, had opened it, and was leaning out into the street.

"I tell you I have seen that face somewhere before," he reiterated.

"So have I," added the Marquis, going to the window as well.

Raymond joined them, and watched the skeleton-like old man across the street He was tracking Huascar, like a little boy playing at brigands, childishly taking ineffective cover behind carts, pedestrians and trees. The Indian had noticed him, and turned once or twice; then continued on his way openly, quite unconcerned.

Suddenly, the Marquis, pensively leaning against the window, straightened himself with an exclamation.

"That is Orellana! The father of Maria-Cristina de Orellana!"

Natividad started.

"You are right. That's who it is... I remember him well now."

They remained as if stunned by this apparition from the terrible past; this ghost come to remind them that he, too, had had a beautiful daughter; that she had vanished ten years before, during the Interaymi, and that he would never see her again. The Marquis, crushed by a flood of old memories, sat inert in an armchair, deaf to Natividad's reassuring words, and refused to touch a mouthful of the meal prepared for them.

Raymond, at the Marquis' exclamation, had dashed down into the street, caught up with the mysterious old man at the corner of the square, and put a hand on his shoulder. The stranger turned, looking at the young man fixedly.

"What do you desire, señor?" he asked in a toneless voice.

"I want to know why you are following that man." Raymond pointed to Huascar, just disappearing at another corner.

"Do you not know, then? The great day of the Interaymi is near. I am following that man because he commands the Red Ponchos, who are taking my daughter to the Cuzco. She is the Bride of the Sun, you know. But this time I shall not let her die! I shall save her, and we will return together to Lima, where her fiancée is waiting. *Adios*, señor!"

He stalked away on his long legs, leaning on the crook.

"Mad!" said Raymond aloud.

Then he clenched his fists as if to hold his own reason. This inaction would drive him insane! To think that in the very heart of a supposedly civilized city there was nothing to do but to wait And wait for what? Huascar's good pleasure; his good pleasure to keep his word or break it. Could he force that house alone? He could at all events try, and fight his way to Marie-Thérèse's feet, even if he was killed the minute afterwards.

He stopped, and pulled himself together.

What good purpose would that serve? No, he must wait; wait until midnight, when Huascar would return. That was the only thing to do; ruse for ruse, and the golden voice of money to talk to those Indians. But midnight was a long way off. Ten times the young man paced around the square, wondering and raging. Surely there were behind all these beflagged and festooned windows a legion of Christian men who would rise like a hurricane if they knew the abominable truth!

Raymond's thoughts were interrupted by the appearance of a dancing, singing, howling mob at the end of the neighboring calle. This, then, was the populace which he would have raised against Garcia, and which obeyed Garcia, while the Dictator, like Pilate, washed his hands of it. The mob approached, to the thunder of drums and bugles, while flaming torches and swaying paper lanterns lit up the scene, for night had now fallen. Overhead fluttered banners adorned with crosses and strange symbols perhaps two thousand years old. Christians, this crowd? Perhaps!

Not a man of the upper classes was to be seen, not even a high-caste Indian. Here were only the dregs of the city; a mass of howling maniacs, whirling and whooping round a huge bonfire which had flared up in the center of the square, their wild yells punctuated by salvas of *cohetes*. On one side of the square, they were singing hymns; on the other, they were drinking, smoking, and swearing. One group of natives swept into a church, still dancing; another entered the theater and became religiously silent, awaiting the arrival of Garcia, for whom a gala was being given.

Raymond, arms crossed and brows knit, glared at the passing groups. There was nothing to be done with such brutes as these! Then he took a sudden resolution. To the four winds with Huascar and his promises! He would go to that little adobe house! Feeling to see if his revolver was safe in his pocket, he turned, only to be confronted by Huascar.

"Señor, where are you going?"

He put a hand on the engineer's arm, restraining him. Raymond roughly shouldered the man away.

"You know where I am going."

Again the Indian intervened.

"Return to the inn, señor," he advised calmly. "I will be there in two hours' time with the little lord. But if you make another step, I cannot answer for the safety of your betrothed."

Huascar's voice had changed as he said "your betrothed." Raymond, looking up quickly, saw nothing but hatred in the Indian's eyes. *Marie-Thérèse is lost*, he thought despairingly. Then a flash of light seemed to illumine the abyss into which he felt himself rolling with her.

"Huascar," he said abruptly, "if you save Don Christobal's daughter..."

He stopped a moment, for his heart was beating as if it would burst. In those few seconds of silence, which seemed an eternity, the barbaric picture of that scene became imprinted on his brain for all time—this dark archway under which they had instinctively drawn, the somber and deserted street before them, the intermittent uproar from the plaza mayor, and, in the adjacent streets, the banging of *cohetes* thrown by mischievous boys under the feet of all that passed. Just opposite, at a window on the first floor, half-a-dozen globules of colored fire flickered in the darkness; a family of royal Arequipenos had been illuminating in honor of Garcia before going to see the torchlight procession, or to the gala at the Municipal Theater.

Raymond waited until an Indian, loaded down with horse-cloths, had passed and vanished; perhaps, subconsciously, he was awaiting the miracle which would render unnecessary what he was about to say. The Indian waited, motionless as a statue.

"If you save her, I swear to you by my God that she shall never be my wife."

Huascar did not answer at once. He was evidently taken by surprise.

"I shall save her," he said at last. "Return to the inn, señor. I shall be there at midnight."

He turned and walked toward the river without another look at Raymond, who made his way back to the plaza mayor, his ears buzzing, convinced that he had freed Marie-Thérèse.

CHAPTER V

Absorbed by his thoughts, shaken by the mental storm through which he had just passed, Raymond did not notice what was happening about him, and was nearly ridden down by a detachment of hussars clearing a way to the theater. The hussars were escorting an open carriage drawn by four splendidly caparisoned horses, and seated in the carriage were two men: General Garcia, in all the glory of the fullest of full uniforms, and beside him, in immaculate evening dress, Oviedo Runtu.

When he saw the Indian, Raymond made as if to rush after the carriage, but he was swept away in a swirl of the crowd and, hardly knowing how, carried right into the theater on that human flood. He at once tried to escape, but could not battle his way back to the door. Garcia, surrounded by a glittering staff, was bowing to the cheering crowd from the front of the presidential box. Raymond was so placed that he could not see Oviedo Runtu. The Indian, modestly hidden behind a column, left Garcia to wrestle with his glory alone.

A French actress, *of the Comédie Française*, if the posters were to be believed, came before the footlights and recited Spanish verse, in which Garcia was hailed as "the Savior of the country."

Then the curtain rose, revealing a pedestal, on which was the bust of a general. It had served several times before for a like purpose, but this time it was supposed to represent Garcia. Around it was grouped the whole company, which intoned a triumphal chorus. Then, one by one, the actors filed past the bust, each with his little speech and a wreath.

146

The bust was almost buried in flowers when an Indian girl appeared. She was wearing the Quichua costume: a little tunic open at the neck, and a dozen skirts of various colors worn one on the other; over her shoulders, a woolen mantlet, secured at the throat by a spoon-shaped brooch.

She was greeted with a roar of delight by the Indian part of the audience. And she, in turn, in order that nothing might be lacking from Garcia's triumph, sang something in Indian, something by which the Indians also put all their hope and trust in the Savior of the Country. At the last verse, she shouted, "Long live Garcia!" tand he crowd took up the cry. There were other voices, however, shouting, "Huayna Capac Runtu!"

A gorgeous din followed. Every Indian in the theater jumped up, cheering, joined by scores of half-breeds who suddenly remembered their descent and, tired of being treated with contempt by the colonizers, joined in the roar of "Long live Huayna Capac Runtu!" The purely Peruvian element sat motionless in stalls and boxes.

Meanwhile, in the presidential box, Garcia had drawn to his constellated bosom the resplendent shirt-front of the bank-clerk, embracing before all the illustrious descendant of the Inca kings. The house, enthusiastic before, became delirious.

The gala was over, and Raymond was carried out of the theater as he had been swept in. He had seen enough to realize how useless had been the Marquis' visit to the Dictator. Garcia was helpless without the Indians, and the real master of the situation was Oviedo. Raymond had now no hope but in Huascar. It was eleven o'clock, and he hurried back to the inn.

There he found Natividad and the Marquis equally anxious at his protracted absence. As to Uncle François, nobody had seen him since the arrival at Arequipa, and nobody worried about him. Raymond told them of his meeting with Huascar; he was convinced now of the Indian's good faith.

They did not exchange another word until midnight, anxiously peering out of the windows for some sign to confirm their hopes. Natividad was as anxious as his two companions. He was a kind-hearted man, and had gone so far into the adventure that he could no longer withdraw without loss of self-esteem. Moreover, he was so compromised, politically speaking, that, all things being considered, he could not do better than stand by the Marquis to the end. Whatever the result, he was sure that Don Christobal would not let him starve.

Midnight came, and the twelve strokes rang out from the church tower.

The theater had long since given up its last enthusiasts, and the square was now more or less deserted. All the paper lanterns had gone out, but the night was a clear one, and they could easily distinguish the shadows moving homewards under the arcades. None of them, though, came toward the inn. A quarter past twelve. Not one of the three men in the room dared say a word!

At half-past twelve, still nothing! The Marquis heaved a strangled sigh. At a quarter to one, Raymond went over to the little lamp smoking on the table, took out his revolver, and opened it to see that it was loaded and working properly.

"Huascar has fooled us like children," he said, vainly striving to control his voice. "He came here in broad daylight, with the knowledge of his accomplices, and threw sand in our eyes. He has kept us quiet for hours that were priceless to them, and might have been to us. I have no hope left. Marie-Thérèse is lost, but I shall see her again if I die for it."

He left the room. Don Christobal, catching up his cloak and arming himself as well, followed, Natividad in his wake. They crossed the square in silence. At the top of the alley leading down to the adobe house, Natividad asked the Marquis what he intended to do against fifty armed men.

"The first man we see will be offered a thousand *soles* to speak. If he refuses, a knife in the ribs. Then we shall see."

When they reached the point where they had been stopped by Civil Guards earlier in the day, they were astonished to find the sentry gone. For a moment, there was a flicker of hope in their hearts, but when they had advanced another twenty yards and saw the house unguarded, they realized the truth. They ran forward and entered the open door. All the rooms were deserted. In one of them they found the same pungent odor as at the hacienda on the Chorillos road.

"They are lost," muttered Natividad, while the Marquis, breaking down at last, called his children's names aloud through the deserted house.

Raymond, exploring the place, fell over a crouching figure, and put all his pent-up rage into throwing the man. Half strangled and trembling with fear, the captured half-breed explained that he was the owner of the house. He had been roistering in the city, but the threat of death sobered him and loosened his tongue.

Just after eleven o'clock, a closed carriage had driven up to the door. He did not know who had entered it, but it had been escorted to the station by all the women and the Red Ponchos. This he knew for certain, because he had followed them out of curiosity. At the station, the man they called Huascar had given him some money, telling him to go away and not to return to the house before daylight.

"The blackguard!" growled Raymond. "He knew we would come here when he didn't turn up! Come on! To the station, quick!"

When they reached it, it was with the greatest difficulty that they finally unearthed an employee asleep on a bench. He made no secret of the fact that a large number of Indians had left at a quarter past eleven, in a special train ordered by Oviedo Runtu "for his servants." No, they could not get another special train that night for all the money in the world. If they wanted to get to Sicuapi as well, they would have to wait until the morning. This said, he returned to his interrupted nap.

That night was a terrible one for the three men. They made another vain attempt to reach Garcia, and then wandered through the streets until dawn. Don Christobal was beginning to talk incoherently, and showed all the signs of approaching dementia. Again and again Raymond led them back to the adobe house and wandered through the empty rooms. The half-breed had taken to his heels.

Natividad was not in a much better condition than his companions, and when the first morning train started, it carried three specters in one compartment. Other travelers, hesitating at the door, literally bolted when they saw their wild eyes.

The train went as far as Sicuani, but they did not reach it the same day, being obliged to pass a night at Juliaca, nearly ten thousand feet above sea level, where they again found the trace of the Red Ponchos. It was intensely cold, and all three were taken with mountain sickness, which made them so weak that they were forced to take some rest.

They only partially recovered next day, at Sicuani. There was a motor service between Sicuani and Cuzco, which was working despite the revolution, but the Marquis, unwilling to trust anybody or anything, bought a car for himself at a fabulous price. He was also moved by the thought that it might prove useful later on.

Just as they were leaving the station road in their new acquisition, they met Uncle François, cool, unperturbed, and fresh as a daisy. An avalanche of questions did not ruffle his calm.

"Well, I lost you at Arequipa and did not know what to do. Then I said to myself, 'They are sure to be somewhere near the Red Ponchos.' We are following them, are we not? So when I saw one, I stuck to him like a leech. I followed him to a little house near the river, which was guarded by soldiers. That, said I to myself, must be where these dear children are being kept prisoners. You did not appear, and I thought you had gone ahead. Everybody knows where these ceremonies take place, I suppose. But I did not, so I stuck to my Red Poncho. When they went to the station, I followed. Somebody told me it was a special train and I couldn't get in, but I gave the guard two *soles* and slept in his van. When we arrived, I couldn't see you anywhere. I went on to Cuzco, but you were not there either. So I came back to meet this morning's train. And here I am!"

Uncle François does not realize to this day how near he came to being strangled by his dutiful nephew, or stabbed by the Marquis. His superb calm nearly drove them frantic.

"Where did they take Marie-Thérèse?" demanded Raymond, roughly, though he owed the unconscious tracker more thanks than blame.

"You know well enough! To the House of the Serpent."

"The House of the Serpent!" Raymond turned, to Natividad, gripping his sleeve. "I have heard you say something about that place. What does it mean?"

"It means that they are in the Antechamber of Death."

BOOK V: THE HOUSE OF THE SERPENT

CHAPTER I

Marie-Thérèse opened her eyes. What was this dream from which she had awakened, or into which she had fallen? Little Christobal's plaintive voice brought her keen realization of the brutal truth. She held out her arms to the child, but felt neither his kisses nor his tears on her face. Her eyes were still heavy with magic sleep, and she opened them with difficulty.

When, gradually, she came out of the abyss of darkness and dreams into which she could be plunged almost instantly by the sacred sachets always ready in the hideous fists of the three living mummies; the mammaconas, too, had terrible perfumes which they burned round her in precious vases, sandia more pungent than incense, more hallucinating than opium, which transformed the Bride of the Sun into a beautiful living statue. Then they could sing their songs uninterruptedly, for Marie-Thérèse had gone to another world, and heard nothing of what happened about her.

Curiously enough, her spirit then carried her back to the hour when the knock had come at her window in Callao and when, dropping the big green ledger to the floor, she had run to meet Raymond. She was worried, too, by the ever-present memory of an unfinished letter to their agent in Antwerp, which she had been writing when that other knock at the window had sent her running to Raymond again. She remembered with horrible distinctness the appearance of the three living mummies, swaying in the darkness, and the feel on her mouth and face of the hands made parchment-like by the eternal night of the catacombs. Waking from this lethargic slumber, she thought she had shaken off a dream, but when her eyes opened, she no longer knew whether she had not just entered into a terrible dreamland.

When Marie-Thérèse opened her eyes this time, she was in the House of the Serpent. She knew, for the mammaconas had told her, that when she awoke there she would be near unto death. There it was that Huayna Capac, father of the last King of the Incas, would come to fetch the bride offered to Atahualpa, and take her with him to the Enchanted Realm of the Sun. In the lucid moments left to her during the voyage, when she was given the nectar that kept her alive, the mammaconas had taught her the duties of the Bride, and the first principles of the faith to which she was to be sacrificed.

At first, Marie-Thérèse had hoped that she would be happy enough to lose her reason, or that the terrible fever which took her would free the troubled soul before the body was taken to martyrdom. But the mammaconas knew the secrets which cure such fevers, and had given her to drink a reddish liquid, chanting the while:

"Fever has spread over you its poisoned robe. The hated conquerors shall never know our secrets, but our love for Atahualpa's bride is greater than our hatred. Drink and be well, in the name of Atahualpa, who awaits thee!"

So she had returned to life, only to die again, and so, a nerveless statue, she had traveled right across Peru, to the little adobe house at Arequipa, the last stopping-place before the House of the Serpent. There she had seen Huascar for the first time, bearing in his arms something covered with a veil. Careless of all the listening ears about her, she had risen, and called to him as to a savior. He had answered:

"Thou belongest to the Sun, but before he takes you, thou shalt have a great joy. Thou shalt see thy little brother again."

Then he lifted the veil and showed her Christobal, sleeping. She had run forward, while he had retreated in terror. None but the appointed may touch the Bride of the Sun, and the three guardians of the Temple were there, armed, and swaying gently. One of them signed to a mammacona, who carried the sleeping boy to his sister; she burst into tears, for the first time since her captivity. The child opened his eyes and clung to her, sobbing, "Marie-Thérèse! Marie-Thérèse!"

"How did he come here? You would not hurt him!"

"We shall do as he wishes. He came to us, not we to him. He himself shall decide his fate. Let him beware of his words. That is all I can say to you, all I can do for you. Is that not so, ye Guardians of the Temple?"

Marie-Thérèse, clutching the child to her, looked at them with fresh terror painted on her features; at Huascar, calm and motionless; at the three living mummies, gently swaying.

"What do you mean? How can a child beware of his words?"

Huascar, without moving, then spoke to little Christobal.

"Child, will you come with me? I will take you to your father."

"No! I will stay with Marie-Thérèse!"

"The child has spoken," said Huascar. "So it is ordered. Is it not so, Guardians of the Temple?"

The three horrible skulls swayed gently.

155

Then Huascar, before leaving, had chanted the words of an Almara psalm:

"Blessed are those who shall come pure to the Kingdom of the Sun, pure as the hearts of little children, at the dawn of the world."

"Huascar, have pity! Remember my mother!"

Huascar bowed to the Guardians of the Temple and went out silently.

Marie-Thérèse, crooning over little Christobal, covered him with kisses.

"Why did you come, little one? Why did you come?"

"To tell you not to be afraid, Marie-Thérèse. Papa and Raymond are coming. They are following, and will save us both. But if you must die, little sister, I will die with you."

The mammaconas, moving silently, had lit the sandia in their precious vases; brother and sister slept together, in each other's arms.

Now she had awakened in the House of the Serpent, and Christobal was not with her. She struggled to regain consciousness, heard his cries nearby, and rose from the cushioned couch on which she had been reclining. There was Christobal, naked, struggling in the hands of the mammaconas. Terrified, she made as if to rush to his assistance, but six of the women surrounded her, calmed her with fluttering hands. No harm would come to the child; he was being dressed, as she would be dressed, in a robe made of bat skins. They spoke with infinite respect, giving her a title she had not heard before; they called her Coya, which, in Inca, means queen.

The mammaconas took her in their powerful arms, lifting her like a child, and took off the sulphur-hued robes with which she had been adorned in the deserted hacienda. Again they anointed her with sweet oils and perfumed creams, chanting the while a slow and restful lullaby, stilling to the senses. They were tall women from the province of Puno, born on the shores of Titicaca, strong and beautiful; their walk was almost rhythmic, supple and harmonious, while their rounded arms showed golden against the black of their veils. They had splendid eyes—all that could be seen of their faces.

Marie-Thérèse and little Christobal were afraid of them, but they were not cruel. Two of their numbers were to die with Marie-Thérèse, to prepare the nuptial chamber in the Palace of the Sun, and they were the most lively, the happiest, the most consoling and understanding. They were wholly happy, and were sad that the Bride did not share that happiness, doing all they could to make her understand the joy of being chosen among all as the Goya. On their ankles they wore great golden bracelets, and in their ears heavy circlets.

The child was no longer crying. They had promised him that if he was good he would return to Marie-Thérèse's arms. She also obeyed the mammaconas docilely. The chant with which they filled her ears lulled her spirit, still heavy with the magic sleep.

There was a thought, too, which gave her courage. Those who were dearest to her knew where she was, what had happened to her, who had carried her off, and why. If little Christobal had been able to find her, surely her father and Raymond could do so. They would both be saved. If Raymond had not appeared before, it was because he delayed until he was sure of success. At any moment they might appear with the police and soldiers, all these savages would vanish in the mountains, and the horrible dream would be ended. She felt as weak as a child face to face with Destiny.

CHAPTER II

"In the Home of the Sun," sang the mammaconas for the hundredth time, "the trees are heavy with fruits, and when they are ripe the branches bend down to the earth, that the Indian need not even raise his hand to pick them. Do not weep! Thou shalt live eternally, eternally! Death knocks at the doors of the earthly palace, and the Spirit of Evil stretches his accursed wings over our forests. Weep not! On high in the heavens, near the Sun and the Moon, who is his sister and his first bride, near Charca, who is his faithful page, thou shalt live eternally, eternally!"

On Marie-Thérèse's perfumed tresses they placed the royal borla, its golden fringe overshadowing her eyes and giving her a strange hieratic beauty. She shivered when the bat-skin robe slipped over her limbs; it was as if she had donned something viscous and icy, which from that instant made her part and parcel of the eternal night of which the bat is Coya.

Then they placed on her wrist a circlet which she recognized as the Golden Sun bracelet. She realized that her last hours had begun, and thought sadly of the happy yet terrible day when this bracelet first appeared in her existence; she remembered the horror-stricken face of Aunt Agnes, the old duenna crossing herself, her father's skepticism and Raymond's loving laugh. Where were they all now? Why did they not come to her rescue?

Marie-Thérèse stretched out her arms to the Providence that seemed to have deserted her, and closed them again on little Christobal, placed in her lap by one of the attendants. When she saw him, clad like herself in the robes of night, she was seized with revolt. This could not be! She turned to the Guardians of the Temple, who came forward in answer to her look, gently swaying. There was no doubt of it! There were the same horrible skulls which Raymond and she had seen taken out of the earth, come from their tombs to take her back with them. But she would speak, and test their mercy. She turned away her eyes, mortally afraid that the steady swaying would overpower her will, and told them she was ready to die quietly, as befitted a Bride of the Sun, if only they would spare the little boy and send him safely back to Lima.

"I will not leave you, Marie-Thérèse! I will not leave you!"

"The child has spoken. So it is ordained."

The Guardians of the Temple exchanged glances and moved away again, gently swaying.

Marie-Thérèse burst into tears, the ring of madness in her high sobs, while the little boy clung desperately, striving to console her.

"Do not cry, Marie-Thérèse! They will come to save us. Papa and Raymond will come... Oh! What was that?"

From behind the walls came the strains of music. A curtain was raised, and the players entered—tall, sad-faced men who took their places in a ring around them. They were the sacred players of the *quenia*, the flute which is made of human bones. Their song was sadder than a *De Profundis*, and Marie-Thérèse shivered, her beseeching eye exploring in vain every corner of the great bare room which was the antechamber of her tomb.

Monstrous, Cyclopean masses of stone, hexagonal in shape and placed one upon the other without mortar, held in place by their mighty weight alone, formed the walls of the House of the Serpent. She knew where she was, for the mammaconas had told her. There were two Houses of the Serpent, one at Cajamarca, the other at Cuzco. They were called thus because of the stone serpent carved over the main entrances. The serpent was there to guard the sacred precincts, and never allowed the victims of the Sun to escape. Aunt Agnes and old Irene had often told her this, and until now, she had always laughed.

Marie-Thérèse, then, was in Cuzco, in a palace well known to travelers, historians, and archaeologists; a place which all may enter, which all may leave in freedom; a place to which guides brought the tourist. Then what did it all mean? Why should she be afraid? Her friends were sure to come to her rescue. But why were they still not here?

Which way would they come? Listen! Yes, above the sad piping of the *quenias* rose other sounds: murmurs, footsteps, and the dull rumble of a gathering throng. It came from over there, from behind that vast curtain, that vast golden-yellow curtain which stretched right across the room and prevented her from seeing. What did it hide, and what was that crowd awaiting?

Marie-Thérèse questioned the two mammaconas who were to die with her. They were stretched at her feet in their long black veils, and rose with respect to answer. The faithful were waiting to adore King Huayna Capac, who would come to lead her back to Atahualpa. Marie-Thérèse, uncomprehending, asked more questions. He would come from the bowels of the earth to claim them, and they would pass through the realms of night in their robes of mourning, till they reach the Enchanted Realm of the Sun. Then they would be clad all in gold, with golden dresses and jewels of gold, for all time.

"And the little boy?" asked Marie-Thérèse.

To her horror, they turned their heads away and did not answer. She caught Christobal more closely to her, covering his face with kisses, as if she wished to smother him with caresses to save him from a more terrible fate. The child strove to console her.

"Do not be afraid," he whispered. "Papa and Raymond will come, not the wicked King. They will soon be here."

On one of the giant stones were mysterious signs to which the whispering mammaconas drew each other's attention—strange sculptured figures with the head of man and the body of the coraquenque. In all time and on all the earth, so say the Incas, there has been only one couple of *coraquenques*, two of the mystic birds which appeared in the mountains at the coronation of each new king and gave him two of their feathers to adorn his head-dress.

Behind the curtain, the noise had ceased, and the song of the *quenias* suddenly grew so piercing that Marie-Thérèse cried out in terror. Christobal, clutching at her bosom, nestled even closer. Then the curtains were parted, and the whole hall was revealed.

A long way below her was a prostrate and silent crowd. On the porphyry steps which stretched down to this crowd stood the three Guardians of the Temple. A step below them, Huascar, his arms crossed under his red poncho. Lower still, four prostrate Red Ponchos, who were the Guards of the Sacrifice. Their heads, completely hidden by the sacred bonnet and ear-caps, were bent so low that none could see their faces.

Surely there was somebody in that huge crowd who would free her! Marie-Thérèse, filled with a wild hope, rose with the child in her arms, and cried for mercy. But the booming answer took away all hope.

"*Muera la Coya! Muera la Coya! To death with the Queen!*"

They gave her the title in Aïmara, but clamored for her death in Spanish, so that she would understand her fate. The four mammaconas on her right, the four others on her left, and the two who were to die with her, surrounded the young girl, forced her back to her seat. But she still struggled, holding up the boy, and begging that he, at least, might be spared.

"He is the sacrifice of Pacahuamac," came the answer.

And the mammaconas, taking up the echo, chanted:

"The sacrifice of Pacahuamac! Before all things began, before the Sun and before the Moon, his sister, was the Great Spirit, Pacahuamac. Pacahuamac, the Great Spirit!"

Down below there, the surging crowd took up the cry. Huascar, turning, commanded silence with a gesture. They were all standing now, except the four Red Ponchos on the last step; still prostrate and silent. The cry of the *quenias* rose again, strident and shrill; soon they alone were to be heard. Marie-Thérèse, crushed, conquered, had ceased struggling. Not a voice, not a sign, had answered the appeal. In a groan, she begged the mammaconas for their perfumes.

"Have mercy. Bring your perfumes. Then we shall not suffer."

The two who were to die with her shook their heads.

"We must go to Atahualpa awake, with our hearts and all our senses, so that we may live hereafter."

The *quenia* players ceased their music, and a terrible, gripping silence descended on the hall. The faithful fell to their knees, and Huascar's sonorous voice commanded silence.

"Silence! Silence in the House of the Serpent! The dead King is coming! Listen!"

It was as if an earthquake had shaken the walls. The place was filled with thunder. But instead of coming from the heavens, it rose from the very bowels of the earth. Little Christobal trembled in his sister's arms, clung closer, and whispered:

"Look, Marie-Thérèse! Look at the Red Ponchos."

She lifted her eyes, looked, trembled, and forced herself to silence. While every other head was bent in worship, the Guards of the Sacrifice had raised theirs, and under the sacred bonnets, despite the stain that disguised them, Marie-Thérèse recognized the faces of Raymond, her father, Natividad and Uncle François.

When she looked a second time, the four bonnets were prostrate again, and a cry from Huascar, herald of Huayna Capac, brought the multitude to its feet.

Another tremor shook the very foundations of the temple, and one wall seemed to vanish.

"Huayna Capac!"

CHAPTER III

That part of the wall on which were sculptured the strange signs and the two human-headed birds had opened, as if on a pivot. Marie-Thérèse cowered and covered her face with her hands, for the dead king was emerging from the gulf of shadow beyond. The wall swung back into position, and the young girl, opening her eyes again, saw before her a two-seated throne of massive gold. The seat on the right of the dead majesty was unoccupied. The great crowd of Indians was bent to the dust in adoration, while the dirge of the quenia-players rose to the roof in ever-increasing volume.

The two mammaconas who were to accompany Marie-Thérèse to the Enchanted Realm of the Sun stood on each side of her, while the ten other priestesses, formed in two lines, passed and re-passed before her, in the intricate steps of a sacred dance. When they came before the Dead One's throne, they fell to their knees, then rose again, chanting:

"This is Huayna Capac, King of kings, son of the great Tapac Inca Yupanqui. He has come by the Corridors of Night to claim the new Coya offered by the Inca people to his son Atahualpa."

Then they moved backwards, crossing and re-crossing, swaying their black veils. Twelve times they repeated this movement, and each time the chant grew louder, while the purl of the *quenias* swelled and broadened.

Marie-Thérèse, holding Christobal closely to her, stared fixedly at Huayna Capac, and the Dead One seemed to stare back at her. He also wore the bat-skin robe made for the Corridors of Night, but beneath it could be seen the royal mantle and the golden sandals. His face, calm and severe, majestic in its still beauty, nearly had the hues of life; it was framed in masses of coal-black hair, crowned with the royal borla in which quivered the plumes of the coraquenque. Under the half-closed lids the eyes seemed living. The dead king was seated naturally, his hands resting on his knees, and so life-like was his whole attitude that to Marie-Thérèse's horrified eyes he seemed to be breathing. Only little Christobal heard her half-strangled cry, for the mammaconas were repeating their chant for the twelfth time, and with the piercing note of the quenias, deadened all other sound in the House of the Serpent.

Down below there, the mob of Indians was swaying, swaying gently from right to left, in imitation of the rhythmic movements of the three Guardians of the Temple. Marie-Thérèse kept her eyes fixed on the dead king, not only because he was just opposite her and, half fascinated, she could not do otherwise, but also because she did not wish to look at the Red Ponchos. She felt that if her eyes were allowed to wander for an instant, they would fatally betray the four.

Marie-Thérèse was now as if half buried in the idea of death; she felt as if the earth had already claimed her, only leaving her head free for a little longer. She was becoming gradually hypnotized by the motionless monarch, while the fanatical crowd about her wondered, awestruck.

Huascar raised his arm, two fingers of his right hand imposing immediate and absolute silence. The Guardians of the Temple drew near, pointing towards the vacant seat on the golden throne. Two mammaconas lifted up Marie-Thérèse, carried her to it, and placed her beside Huayna Capac, son of the great Tapac Inca Yupanqui. Then the double throne was turned until it faced the assembly and the Red Ponchos.

Marie-Thérèse closed her eyes, shivering at the thought of the corpse beside her. She dared not open them, realizing with horrible distinctness that if she did she must try to run down to Raymond, or call out something that would betray them. Though her eyes were closed, and she outwardly seemed as dead as the mummy beside her, Marie-Thérèse knew what was happening. Little Christobal, peeping over the curve of his sister's arms, was watching everything, and a whisper, so low that she hardly felt the breath rising along her bare neck, said:

"Raymond has lifted his head... Papa is looking at us... we must not move."

Marie-Thérèse pressed her trembling fingers on the child's lips, and he was silent. Her tired brain, working, wondered what they were going to do. It was horrible to know them there, hidden and helpless. For if they had not been helpless, they would not be hidden, they would have come with police and soldiers. Could it be that the Indians were masters of the country now? Then she thought of the revolution, of Garcia, who had once loved her. Why had they not gone to him? At a word, he would have come with his whole army. And they, hidden under their ponchos, what could they do? What was their plan?

The mammaconas were chanting:

"Earthquakes shook the world. The moon was girdled with rings of many colors. Thunder fell on the royal palace, and reduced it to ashes. An eagle, hard pursued by falcons, circled over the great square of the city, filling the heavens with his cries. Pierced by the talons of his foes, he fell dead at the feet of the noblest among the Incas."

At these words, recalling the defeat and death of their last ruler, all bent their heads, groaning, and the breath of the *quenia* players trembled in the dead men's bones. Huascar had also bent to the ground; then he raised his forehead and his eyes met those of Marie-Thérèse. She shivered, and when he moved toward her, she thought her last hour had come. She had been able to appeal to the mercy of the crowd, but she could not call to this man, whose look showed that he loved her. She closed her eyes.

Huascar's voice reached her, slow, cadenced, and monotonous.

"Coya, thou belongest to Huayna Capac, the great King who will take thee to the House of the Sons of the Sun. We leave thee alone with him. He will lead thee through the Corridors of Night, which no living man must know, and in the temple will seat thee among the Hundred Wives. Thou must obey him, thou must rise only if he rises! Thou must obey. And remember that the serpent watches in the House of the Serpent."

He withdrew, still facing her, with the three Guardians of the Temple, while the great crowd below flowed silently through the three doors.

All the mammaconas followed, drawing their black veils over their faces, like widows leaving a cemetery. Even the two who were also to die left her, first bending to kiss her feet, peeping shoeless from under the bat-skin robe.

Darkness was rapidly gaining the hall. Why were they leaving her alone there? What was this horror which even they dared not see? She must not rise unless he rose. Would this dead thing come to life, then, take her by the hand, and lead her into the eternal night? What of the Red Ponchos? She looked. They were still there, prostrate at the foot of the steps. The Guards of the Sacrifice, she had heard them called. They were stopping! A surge of joy filled her heart. She felt less afraid now.

The Guardians of the Temple had left. Huascar had left. Would the Red Ponchos follow? No, they did not move. She was watching them now, with her whole soul. They were still there, motionless, ready to spring to her rescue when the hall was empty, ready to carry her to the horses that must be waiting. The Dead One at all events could do nothing to prevent it.

There were only twenty Indians left in the hall now... only five... four... three... They turned slowly at the doorway to look at her again... She sat motionless, rigid... She must not move unless the Dead One moved... Only the four Red Ponchos remained... She half screamed... They also had risen, pacing slowly toward the doors.

It could not be! They could not be deserting her! But they were going away like the others, without looking in her direction. No, she must not scream... she must wait patiently... wait for a sign. Still walking slowly, three of them had gone to the three doors, but the fourth, Raymond, turned suddenly, his finger on his lips.

Forgetting Huascar's words, Marie-Thérèse half rose in her seat. There was a revolver in Raymond's fist now, and her father had vanished through one of the doors, looking to make sure that the courtyard was deserted. Then his voice gave the signal:

"*Recuerda!*" (Remember!)

Raymond dashed up the porphyry steps, Don Christobal following, while the two others remained at the doors.

"Come, Marie-Thérèse! Quick!"

Raymond stretched out his hands to take little Christobal, and Marie-Thérèse had risen, when a terrible whistling sound filled the hall, and the two prisoners, shrieking, were hurled back into the seat by the monstrous folds of a huge serpent which seemed to spring into life about them, binding them down to the throne of Death. The serpent of the House of the Serpent had come to claim his prey.

Raising his revolver, Raymond thundered at the hideous head towering above them, whistling with wide-open jaws, and tore at the coils which imprisoned his fiancée. His hands fell, not on living flesh, but on hard, cold metal; copper rings which ground one against the other, overlapped, and drew tighter. It was in vain that he and Don Christobal tore at them with furious hands.

"Look out! They are coming!" shouted Natividad from the doorway.

The hall was invaded by Indians, while the Serpent shrieked stridently, and a thousand rattles seemed to sound the alarm. The Marquis still tore at the coils that were choking his children, but Raymond, hesitating a moment, dashed down the stairs. In a twinkling, the hall was full of Indians, priests, caciques, mammaconas, scores of Quichua soldiers from the train of Oviedo Runtu, who alone remained invisible.

Huascar appeared, still calm and immovable, as if this scene did not surprise him, as if nothing could surprise him. Had he known beforehand what was to have happened, he could not have given his orders more deliberately. Don Christobal, Natividad, and Uncle François were tied up in a trice, the latter at last alarmed by the brutality of his captors. Raymond had disappeared.

"Take them away," ordered Huascar.

Don Christobal struggled, turned and looked once again.

"Marie-Thérèse! Christobal!"

Then he too was hurried away.

Meanwhile Huascar, more and more somber, directed the search for Raymond. They hunted in vain; he had disappeared like a drop of water in the sea. Finally, Huascar gave the order to clear the hall again.

Left alone with the Guardians of the Temple, who stood caressing the serpent's folds with their hideous little hands, the high-priest went behind the throne. In a moment, the brazen monster was silent, loosened its grip, and shrank link by link, until it vanished whence it had come.

Going to the wall, Huascar placed his hand on the coraquenque, and the massive stones rolled back; the throne shook, slipped backwards, and vanished down the Corridors of Night, taking with it the dead King, Marie-Thérèse and little Christobal, both unconscious. The wall closed upon them, hiding again the secrets which only those who are ready to die may know.

The Guardians of the Temple bent their monstrous heads in obeisance before Huascar, and in their turn went out Huascar, last High Priest of the Incas, was alone in the House of the Serpent Slowly going to the top of the porphyry steps, he sat down. His head dropped between his hands, and there he remained till dawn.

CHAPTER IV

Raymond, clear of the House of the Serpent by what was little short of a miracle, crouched down in a niche of the palace wall, hewn out by some dead Inca hand, and there waited for Huascar throughout the night, watching the door at which he must appear. He was careless of the danger he ran, and his very boldness saved him. Not one of the passing Quichuas, dignitaries of the Interaymi, dreamed for an instant that the poor Indian wrapped in his poncho, and apparently asleep, was the sacrilegious stranger who had slipped from their clutches. The darkness, too, favored him, as it had favored his daring escape; he had merely turned his red poncho inside out, so that it looked like any other poncho, and had joined the howling crowd, stopping in it until Huascar's order had cleared the hall.

Argue the matter as he would, the young man saw no hope. Garcia's victory over the Federal troops at Cuzco had given the district into the hands of the Indians. The Spanish population, only an eighth of the 50,000 souls in the ancient city, had fled. Never since the Spanish Conquest had the Quichuas so completely been the masters. Garcia himself had prudently left the town, waiting for the end of the Interaymi; and the few troops he had left behind him were heart and soul with the native population, from which they had been levied, and with which they shared customs, faith and fetichism. In a word, the Cuzco was as much the home of the Incas as it had been in the heyday of their despotic rulers.

When Raymond and his companions had reached the outskirts of the city they had hidden their car in a half-deserted country inn, bribing the landlord. They had at once realized that force was out of the question. Happily, there remained Garcia's money. The landlord, a poor half-breed who asked no better than to become rich, had listened readily, and the offer of a small fortune had set him off looking for Red Ponchos willing to betray Huascar.

He found four, the very men who were to be the Guards of the Sacrifice, in the House of the Serpent. When these men had explained their functions, the four Europeans could hardly believe their good fortune. Raymond and Don Christobal were so absorbed by the idea of getting through to the prisoners somehow, that they did not stop to think how suspiciously easy their task had been. Uncle François, a witness of the bargain, was for once not altogether wrong when he shrugged his shoulders at their childish scheme to "take him in."

The Red Ponchos agreed to everything, and the price was fixed, and they received half-payment. The remainder was to be handed over when the Marquis' children were free. The traitors promised to help them escape from the sacred precincts, and moreover brought them their disguises.

Uncle François, chuckling covertly, accepted the part assigned to him with such readiness, showed such quiet courage in his attitude, that he reconquered at one stroke the lost esteem of both the Marquis and his nephew. Natividad, ever ready to believe anything to the discredit of an Indian, and knowing from experience how easily they were to be bought, was quite confident in the success of the expedition.

Thoroughly fooled by Huascar, they had walked into the trap, and only amazing luck had saved one of them. Where were the others now? Where was the dungeon that held them, and what was to be their fate?

Raymond was waiting in the dark street before the palace, determined to shoot Huascar when he saw him. All night through, nobody came out of the House of the Serpent. At dawn, the young engineer suddenly felt a hand on his arm, and, looking up, recognized the old man to whom he had spoken at Arequipa, the father of Maria Cristina de Orellana.

"Why do you stop here?" asked the stranger. "You won't see the procession if you do. Follow me, and I'll show you my daughter coming out of the Corridor of Night."

Raymond stared at him. Groups of Indians were passing, all heading in the same direction. The old man spoke again.

"You may as well go with them. They are all off to see the procession of the Bride of the Sun."

Raymond followed him mechanically. Why not, after all? He was nearly mad himself. Why should a madman not be his guide? As they walked, Orellana babbled on tonelessly.

"I know you well. You want to see the Bride of the Sun. I see you have even disguised yourself as an Indian to do so. Not in the least necessary, I assure you. You'll see her, right enough, if you come with me. I know Cuzco, below ground and above ground, better than any living man. I have lived in their secret passages for ten years. When I am not underground, I guide strangers through the city, and show them where the Bride of the Sun used to pass on her way to the Temple of Death. You know that, of course? It's the same as the Temple of the Sun, only underneath. I'll show it you, for it's worth seeing.

"Fine *fêtes* this year, señor. Last time, they had to hide themselves in the Corridors of Night, but today they are masters both above and below, and that dead king of theirs, Huayna Capac, will see daylight again. They'll take him all through the city, as they used to do. If you don't know that, you haven't been keeping your ears open.

"Where are your friends? I could have shown it to them as well. And I don't charge much; a few *centavos* keep me going for weeks. All the innkeepers know me, and send for Orellana when they have visitors. I know you all quite well. I saw you at Mollendo, then at Arequipa, and now here you are again outside the House of the Serpent. That's where they always go first. Yes, that's the way they brought Maria Cristina ten years ago. She was the prettiest girl in Lima, so they chose her for their god. I didn't know then, but this time they won't have their way quite so easily. When I saw the Interaymi come round again, I said to myself: 'Orellana, you must get ready for them.' And I'm ready for them, never fear!"

Thus they crossed the whole city. Raymond, walking like a man in a dream, following to the next station in the martyrdom of his sweetheart, paid no heed to the wonderful ruins on all sides of him, the mighty buildings piled rock on rock by demi-gods, and which have not moved, nor will move until the earth dies, long after the winds of heaven and the quivering of the mountains have stamped flat the miserable huts left by the Conquistadors.

They left the city behind them and Orellana, taking Raymond by the hand, like a little child, made him climb the mount which the Quichuas call the Hill of the Dancing Monkey. Its gigantic summit, hewn into terraces, galleries and giant stairways by long-dead craftsmen, was already crowned with Indians. All eyes were turned toward that other miracle of Inca work which is Sacsay-Huaynam, a hill of stone fashioned into a Cyclopean fortress, with three lines of defenses rising one above the other, each wall dotted with niches from which on this day, as of yore, armed sentries looked out over the country. On the summit of Sacsay-Huaynam towered the Intihuatana, or "the pillar on which the sun is bound."

Orellana's broken voice explained it all to Raymond, guide-like.

"This pillar, señor, was used by the Incas to measure time. A religious stone, erected to mark the exact period of the equinoxes. That is why they call it Intihuatana; it means 'where the sun is bound.' Look over there! You can see the procession starting... Don't you understand? The Corridors of Night run right under the city, from the House of the Serpent to Sacsay-Huaynam. When my daughter comes out, they will take her round the hill, and round the Intihuatana. Then, when the Sun has been freed by the High-Priest, the procession will come down to the gates of the city."

Raymond could now clearly see the procession forming up on the walls, and even distinguished Huascar at its head, giving orders. Leaving Orellana, he hurried toward Sacsay-Huaynam, getting as near as the press of Indians would allow. He could now see that the solstice pillar, placed in the center of a circle, was loaded with festoons of flowers and fruit, while on its summit stood a golden throne. The throne of the Sun, vanished centuries before, had been brought out from the Corridors of Night and replaced there before the dawn.

There was silence on Sacsay-Huaynam; a few priests were grouped round the Pillar, waiting for the hour of noon. Then Huascar appeared, clad in golden vestments. Facing the throne of the Sun, the High Priest waited a few seconds, turned and cried aloud in Aïmara a phrase which was taken up on all sides in Quichua and Spanish:

"The god is seated on the Column in all his light!"

Then he struck his hands together, giving the signal for all to march; the god, having visited his people, had been freed, and continued his voyage through the heavens. The faithful followed him on earth, from east to west. The sacred procession sprang into life, led by Huascar.

First came a hundred servitors of the god, simply dressed, whose task it was to clear the way, chanting paeans of triumph. After them, a group of men in checker-board tunics of red-and-white, whom the populace greeted with shouts of *"The amautas! The amautas!"* (the sages). Then others all in white, bearing hammers and maces of silver and copper, who were the apparitors of the royal palace; the guards and the Inca's body attendants, their azure robes blazing with precious metals; finally, the nobles, with heavy ear-rings marking their rank. The procession wound slowly down from Sacsay-Huaynam to the plain, and then the double throne, borne on the shoulders of the noblest among the Indians, appeared to the multitude. Thousands of throats greeted the dead king and his living companion; a roar of mingled enthusiasm for the descendant of Manco Capac, and hatred for the conquering race, translated by deafening shouts of *"Muera la Coya! Muera la Coya!"*

Marie-Thérèse seemed to hear nothing; pale as marble and beautiful as a statue, she passed unheeding, little Christobal still in her arms. Instead of the bat-skin robes, they now wore vicuna tunics, sheer as silk. Behind them walked the two mammaconas who were to die, their faces veiled with black; the other women and the three Guardians of the Temple had disappeared. The cortège was brought up by a company of Quichua soldiers in modern uniform, rifle on shoulder, tramping to the lilt of the quenia-players, who closed the march.

The contrast between this antique procession and that fragment of a modern army was more than curious. Uncle François, the only one who could have really appreciated it under the circumstances, was not there. As to Raymond, he was watching Marie-Thérèse with the fixed gaze of a madman. Strive as he would, he could get no nearer, and so backed out of the press to run toward the gates of the city, where he hoped to fight his way to the front ranks.

On the last steps of the Hill of the Dancing Monkey he was immobilized by the press of people and forced to look with them to the summit of Sacsay-Huaynam, where, on the top of the highest tower, had appeared the scarlet figure of a priest, sharp-cut against the azure of the sky.

Raymond at once recognized the Preacher of Cajamarca, and voices around him further explained that this was the chief officer of the *quipucamyas*, or Keepers of the Historical Word. His voice, sweeping down from Sacsay-Huaynam, checked the advance of the procession, chanted the glory of by-gone days.

Ringing clear and impassioned, it recalled the day when the Stranger and his diabolical train had first entered those plains after the death of Atahualpa. As to-day, the Sun blazed over the Imperial City, then full of altars sacred to his cult. Then, innumerable buildings, which the conqueror was to leave in ruins, traced white streets in the heart of the valley, and clustered on the

177

lower slopes of the hills. In the conquerors' train was Manco, descendant of kings, in whose name he gave orders and was obeyed. On that day, when the sun went down behind the Cordilleras, it might well have been thought that the Empire of the Incas had ceased to exist.

"But it still lives!" thundered the voice. "The Sun still shines on his children; the Andes, cradle of our race, still tower to the skies; Cuzco, navel of the earth, still quivers at the voice of his priests; Sacsay-Huaynam and the Intihuatana are still standing; the procession of the Interaymi still starts from these sacred walls!"

At these words, the procession moved on again, and had it not been for the anachronism of the riflemen bringing up the rear, one could almost have believed that five hundred years had brought no change in the plains of the Cuzco.

Raymond, finally free to move on, was despairing of ever getting nearer to Marie-Thérèse when he met Orellana again.

"What are you looking for?" asked the old man. "A place to see from? Then come with me, and I'll show you my daughter. I know Cuzco better than the Incas themselves. Come with me."

Once again Raymond allowed the madman to be his guide. They reentered the city by way of the Huatanay ravine, spanned to this day by the Conquistadors' bridges, and entered a maze of side-streets free from the crowd. Skirting the prodigious Hatun Rumioc, or wall-which-is-of-one-rock, they passed Calcaurpata, which tradition makes the palace of Manco Capac himself, first King of the Incas and founder of Cuzco; then they turned toward the Plaza Principale, called Huàcaypata by the Quichuas of today as by the Incas of yore. To reach it, Orellana took Raymond through the ruined palace of the

Virgins of the Sun, detailing, as he went, the uses and names of the various rooms. The young man's impatient interruptions left him quite unmoved.

"We have plenty of time. You shall see my daughter from so near that you could speak to her. Stop a minute, and listen to the quenias. The head of the procession has no more than reached San Domingo. That church, curiously enough, was built on the very foundations of the Temple of the Sun... I have never met a visitor less curious than you are... This is the cloister of the Brides of the Sun... It has always been the home of virtue and piety, for the Christians turned it into a convent under the auspices of Santa Catarina."

Raymond, unable to stand the guide's jargon any longer, began to run toward the noise of the advancing procession.

"You might pay me!" shouted Orellana in his wake. "Pay me what you owe me!" and stooped to pick up the centavos which the young engineer threw on the ground.

Nearing the plaza principale, Raymond again found his way blocked by the crowd, and forgot his anger in the relief of finding a friend when Orellana tugged at his poncho again.

"You might as well stop with me," urged the old man. "Hurrying won't help you. I know a little tiny Corridor of Night that will lead us to the Sun, right to the top stone of one of those temples... It's a temple dedicated to Venus... They call her Chasca, or the young man with the long and curly locks, and he's supposed to be the page of the Sun. Come with me."

Orellana had taken Raymond by the hand, and led him to a cellar, in which they found the foot of a narrow staircase. Once at the top of it, they were, as the old man had promised, on the summit of a ruined temple, dominating the crowded square below and the streets radiating to it like the spokes of a wheel to the huh. Around them were other ruins; temples sacred to the moon, to the "armies of the heavens," which are the stars, to the rainbow, lightning and thunder... walls which still defied the elements, though the temples were now shops, workrooms or stables.

The head of the procession had appeared, the hundred servitors of the god pressing back the crowd, and slowly wound its way round the square. Then the golden litter came into sight and Huayna Capac, for the first time in centuries, came to the center of the world, the Umbilicus of which he had been lord and master. All heads were bowed before this sovereign shadow and the memory of ancient glories once again brought to life. The crowd even forgot for the moment its hatred of the stranger woman, the motionless Coya with the stranger child in her arms.

The double throne was brought to the center of the square, and the crowd rose with clamoring voices. Around the litter, the caciques and the chiefs, the nobles and the amautas, who are the sages, joined hands and began to circle, dancing as they danced of yore, when each man held a link of the golden chain and danced the Dance of the Chain. Hands made the links to-day, for when the Strangers slew Atahualpa, the nobles of the Cuzco threw that chain, which otherwise would have gone to the King's ransom, into the deepest water of Lake Titicaca.

"*Recuerda!*"

Suddenly, as if from the heavens, this cry checked the rhythm of the Dance of the Chain. Marie-Thérèse started on her throne, remembering the signal in the House of the Serpent. The child in her arms also lifted its head, and their eyes questioned the blue vault above from which this word of hope had fallen.

"That was Raymond's voice, Marie-Thérèse! I told you he would come to save us!"

The girl's eyes explored the towering walls about her, black with Indians. How could she recognize him in that crowd? Where was he? Again the voice rang out over their heads, so loud that it could be heard by the most distant unit of the crowd.

"*Recuerda!*"

Every head was turned upwards, and a threatening murmur rose from that human mass, torn from its dream of renascence and liberty by a single Spanish word. *Recuerda!* What must they remember? That they were slaves? That these *fêtes*, striving to recall an abolished past, could only last the space of a day? That the sun of tomorrow, forgetting that of today, would only shine anew on their servitude?

Marie-Thérèse started up from the golden throne with the child in her arms, brought to life and action again by the beloved voice.

Looking higher, they at last saw, on the highest stone in the azure, a pigmy figure holding out its arms to the Coya, and crying, "Marie-Thérèse! Marie-Thérèse!"

"Raymond!"

Then all understood that on high there was a stranger, one of the hated race, come to rob them of the soul of their Coya.

CHAPTER V

Pandemonium reigned in the square. This was sacrilege unspeakable! Did not the Coya already belong to the gods! *Muera la Coya!* Death to the stranger! There was a huge rush, a scramble of raging Indians along parapets, over rocks and the ruins of temples, while the golden litter was hurried away by the Guards of the Sacrifice and the *amautas*. Marie-Thérèse closed her eyes, carrying to the tomb that supreme farewell which was perhaps to cost Raymond his life.

"You must be mad," said the madman Orellana, when he saw Raymond lean over and call to Marie-Thérèse, and when she answered, asked almost angrily: "How did you come to know my daughter?"

The roar of the angry crowd surged up to them, surrounded them, and drew nearer. It was with the greatest difficulty that Orellana shook Raymond out of his strange torpor, dragged him through the gap from which they had emerged, and finally to the labyrinth below the Temple. Apparently familiar with every twist and turning of the place, he led him through a mile of passages, their darkness relieved here and there by round, square or triangular patches of light sifting down between thousand-year-old stones from the world above. Occasionally he stopped to tell Raymond what temple, what palace, they were passing under.

"Yaca-Huasi, which they also call the House of the Serpent, is over our heads now."

"Perhaps they have taken her there!"

"No, no! That's against all the rules. The Temple of Death is the next place."

"Where are we going to? Where are you taking me?"

"To the Temple of Death, of course!"

Raymond followed him without another word, but expressed his surprise when they emerged into the open country.

"Where is the Temple, then?" he asked.

"On the Island of Titicaca. You needn't be afraid. We shall get there before them."

They hired horses at a wayside inn and rode to Sicuani. Here they took a train which, turning onto a branch line at Juliaca, then ran to Puno, on the shores of Lake Titicaca. On the way, Orellana babbled ceaselessly about the country through which they were passing and the ceremony they were to witness.

No stranger has ever seen it. But he, Orellana, asked nobody's permission, and since his daughter was to be wedded to the Sun, it was the least of things that he should be present at the marriage, and particularly as he had planned it all so carefully! It had taken him years to find the Temple of Death, but with patience all things could be done. There was not one dried up river bed underground, not a deserted gold mine which he did not know so well that he could find his way about it with his eyes shut.

And what fortunes he had discovered under the earth; a fortune equal to all the fortunes on earth! It was obvious that the Incas must have got their gold somewhere. Well, he had discovered where! There was plenty of it left, plenty of it left! One day, some clever young engineer would find out, and he would only have to stoop to be as rich as Croesus.

A bitter smile from the young engineer, whose thoughts were far from such things.

But he, Orellana, did not give a fig for all the gold in creation. He loved only his daughter, whom the Indians had taken to the Temple of Death, and it was only the Temple of Death which he had sought.It had taken him years, but now everything was; ready and he was going to save her. He had waited long enough to kiss her again! Ten whole years!

So the old man wandered on, while Raymond listened eagerly, striving to guess how much was truth, and how much madness.

"But how do they get from Cuzco to the Temple of Death?"

"Don't you worry about that... By the Corridors of Night, by the Corridors of the Mountains of Night, by the Corridors of the Lake of Night... By the way, do you know anything about fishing?"

Raymond did not have time to answer this extraordinary question, for the guard had come through to their carriage, and was inviting them to the luggage-van to see the samacuena danced. Everybody else seemed to be going there, and they accepted so as not to draw attention to themselves. They found the van peopled with Indians, dancing, playing the guitar, and drinking hard. At each step, the guard, to celebrate Garcia's victories, fired a volley of cohetes, the mountains throwing back the echo of the explosions.

Then some of the Quichua soldiers in the train gave themselves up to the pleasures of the chase. Spying flocks of *vicuñas* in the hills, they went to the observation-car and tried their luck. One of them, something of a marksman, brought down a *vicuña*, the train stopped with a grinding of brakes, and the guard himself went off to retrieve the bag.

Raymond, wild with impatience, would have liked to club the engine driver and take charge of the locomotive himself, but Orellana calmed him down.

"We're sure to get there before them. You'll see! Why, we shall even have time to do some fishing!"

Leaving their fellow travelers to cut up the *vicuña*, they returned to their carriage, where the stove had been lighted. It had become intensely cold, for they were now in the snow regions, more than fourteen thousand feet above sea level. *Soroche*, or mountain fever, threw the young engineer, and after bleeding violently at the nose, he fell into a semi-comatose condition. He did not recover until Punho, when he again remembered the horrible nightmare through which he was living, and savagely demanded to be shown the way to the Temple of Death.

"We're going there," replied his strange guide, but first took him to the main square, where about a hundred Indian girls, wearing skirts of a dark material and the low-cut bodices of their race, squatted in orderly rows, selling fruits and vegetables dried in the cold.

"There are usually two hundred of them," explained Orellana, "but the Red Ponchos have been this way and chosen the best-looking half for the ceremony. It's the same thing every ten years."

He made a few purchases with Raymond's money, and after adding a flask of *pisco* to his stores, led the way out of the city. At nightfall they reached a huge marsh, alive with water fowl. Next they crossed a heath, llamas and alpacas fleeing at their approach, and finally came to a dismal little bay on the shores of the lake.

Titicaca, in its mountain cradle, is the highest lake in the world. That night, its waters looked somber and heavy, almost dead. A storm, growling in the distance, soon swept down on them with a howl of rain, the waves dashing up the beach mountain-high, and the lightning touching the surrounding peaks with fire.

"Splendid, splendid," muttered Orellana as the storm broke. "That means fine weather for tomorrow. In the meantime, we may as well have supper."

He had led the young man under a giant monolith, hewn to the shape of a door. In a niche of it, Orellana managed to light a dung-cake fire, and here they ate a little and warmed themselves with generous pulls at the pisco flask. Raymond at last fell asleep, while the old man covered him with a horse blanket and paternally watched over his slumbers.

Just before dawn, Raymond awoke to find Orellana reminiscent.

"This place has always brought me luck since I started to look for my daughter, but I cannot make out who to thank for it. Do you know who this god is?"

He pointed to the bas-reliefs which covered the stone. They represented a human being, the head adorned with allegorical rays, and each hand holding a different scepter. Around this being were symmetrically ranged other figures, some with human faces, others with the heads of condors, all holding scepters, and all facing toward the center.

"There's no doubt about it," mused Orellana aloud. "This is nothing like the Incas' work. It is much more sculptural, and much older. There must have been worlds on these shores before the advent of the Incas. They're only savages who steal children... Well, come on. We may as well go out in my boat and meet the sun."

In a little creek, half hidden by rushes, they found a cane pirogue, in which Orellana had soon hoisted a mast and a mat sail.

"Come on," he said, "we'll do some fishing. It's all on the way to the Temple of Death."

Raymond followed him into the fragile craft, and they started for the islands. These came into sight late in the afternoon, a blue blur on the horizon. To Raymond's fevered imagination, they seemed like threatening shadows on the face of the waters, ghostly guardians of the Temple of Death.

Orellana refused to go any nearer that night, hauled down the sail, and threw overboard a heavy stone to anchor his boat. Then he handed Raymond a fishing-rod. At his astonished look, the madman replied:

"People come to the islands to fish, because these waters are blessed by the gods and the catches are better than anywhere else. Can't you do what everybody else does?"

He pointed across the waters to little lights flaring up at the bows of other pirogues, in which sat motionless fishermen.

"All those Indians are fishing," he said. "You may as well join them. If you can't, go to sleep, and don't worry us. You'll see something worthwhile when you wake up."

Orellana woke Raymond just before dawn. The last stars were paling in the heavens at the approach of their King. The deep waters of the lake showed uniformly gray, not a light and not a shadow upon them. Not a sound to break stillness, not a breath of wind in the air. Suddenly, in the Orient, the mountain peaks were touched with fire, a giant furnace sprang into being behind the torn curtain of the Cordilleras, and the sun painted scarlet splashes into the shadows of the sacred islands.

When they pass before the largest of them, which is Titicaca, the Indian fishermen in their fragile pirogues never fail to chant the Aïmara Hymn of the Ancestors, for it was from this island, untold years ago, that sprang the founders of the Inca race in the persons of Manco Capac and Mama Cello, husband and wife, brother and sister, both children of the Sun. Coming in sight of the island, the traveler perceives giant ruins and great masses of rock piled up in an inexplicable manner, so strange that science has not yet been able to give them a date. These are the baths, the palaces and temples of the first Incas.

Raymond, staring landwards from the pirogue, hardly knew whether he was awake or dreaming. Was this a hallucination born of the terrors of the week, or did his eyes really reveal what other eyes had first adored centuries before, at the dawn of the Inca world? As the shadows of night drew away and the island stood out above the waters in all its terrestrial grandeur, he did not merely see dead stones, lifeless temples, and deserted palaces; the Cyclopean whole was peopled by a vast throng, motionless and silent, its myriad faces turned to the flaming Orient. This immobility and silence were those of a dream; there were thousands there who seemed to live and breathe only in the expectation of some mysterious and sacred event.

The disc of the sun was still hidden behind the Andes, but all Nature heralded its approach; the flanks of the mountains were jeweled with a thousand dazzling stones, brooks and torrents were afire, and the broad bosom of the lake was a roseate mirror bearing the still reflections of palaces and temples. Virgins, bearing, as of old, the most beautiful flowers of the season and the emblems of their religion, peopled the porticoes. At the summits of towers, luminous with the dawn, priests waited for their god to show his face.

Suddenly, he appears... he rises... he blazes down on his empire, and is hailed by a great roar.

"Hail, O Sun, King of the Heavens, father of men!"

Earth trembles, waters shiver, the heavens even quiver at the call.

"Hail, O Sun, father of the Inca!"

Arms are stretched toward him, hands heavy with offerings implore his intercession, and every voice chants his glory.

"Hear thy children! Hail, O Sun!"

Cries and songs of triumph are swelled by the clamor of barbaric instruments, and the tumult grows as the radiant disc climbs higher in the heavens, bathing the multitude in light.

"Sun, behold thy Empire! After so many centuries, the faithful, the men who labor in valley and mountain, are still here, and still do thee obeisance. The golden-armed virgins have poured libations from the sacred vases, and the hymns of the priests, after having risen to the heavens, now seem to plunge into the earth."

What is this miracle? The dream has vanished; vanished as do the light mists of morning before the first rays of the sun.

BOOK VI: THE TEMPLE OF DEATH

CHAPTER I

Raymond rubbed his eyes. What had become of that crowd? Who had hailed the god of Day? Now that the sun was high on the horizon, and that things had taken on their true shapes again, he could see only ruined palaces and solitude.

Orellana had driven his pirogue to the shore, and jumped onto the beach, signing to the young man to follow. As they neared the cliffs, he stopped him; the pious throng had vanished, but not in a dream, for the sound of chanting could still be heard from within the rock.

"Come with me," said the old man. "They have gone to the Temple of Death, but we shall be there before them."

They entered a grotto. Raymond had no will but Orellana's, and no hope. He was convinced that Marie-Thérèse would die, and regarded that last greeting of theirs as the supreme one. Once certain that she had passed to the realms of night, he would follow her there. He had been told she was to end her life in the Temple of Death, and this old man, who ten years before had lost his daughter in the same way, said he knew where it was. Well, he would follow him.

The grotto was a deep one. After walking for a few seconds over sand and shells, the old man lit a resinous torch, and the spluttering flame showed the dark entrance of a passage. Before entering it, however, he bent down in a corner and picked something up. Raymond saw that it was a pick.

"What are you going to do with that?"

"Save my daughter, of course! Just come with me, and I'll show you. I shan't let those devils choke her as they did ten years ago. They wall them up alive, you see. All we need do is to wait until they have gone, and then take her out again. Clear enough, isn't it? When I discovered the Temple of Death and saw all the slabs on the wall, I said to myself: 'It would have been easy enough to save her if I had been there.' It was too late then. And of course, I didn't know which stone she was behind. This time, though, I shall watch them... We'll get the best of them yet. See if we don't!"

There was hope, then! Raymond took a long breath, and steadied himself. Madmen with their set ideas are sometimes nearer the truth than sane men with their set reason. Raymond took the pick, and followed Orellana down the winding passage, the torch in the old man's trembling hand throwing weird lights and shadows on their path. There was not a foreign sound to be heard. The earth had choked all noise as it might yet choke them.

Hacked through the stone, their corridor opened at intervals onto little square rooms, probably the burial-places of long-forgotten priests and dignitaries, slumbering there as their brethren of ancient Egypt slumber in the Pyramids. In the last of these rooms, Orellana put out the torch, and fell on his knees, for the narrow gut which they now entered was far too low for a man to stand upright in. A few yards further on, they came to a spacious niche, and stood up again.

"We are there," said the old man, stopping Raymond.

It was far less dark here, and Raymond, his eyes growing used to the obscurity, realized that a diffused light was reaching them from somewhere. The shadowy outline of columns and cornices gradually took shape, and he realized that he was looking down from a height of several feet into a vast hall.

"That is the Temple of Death," said Orellana. "Listen!"

From the distance came the sound of rhythmic chanting, and suddenly a blinding stream of light descended into the chamber before them. Instinctively, they threw themselves back into the darkest corner of their niche. Above them, at the summit of the vast subterranean hall, a stone had been removed, letting in the golden sunlight. In the heart of the vault was a kind of truncated cone, so fashioned that the sunbeams, sliding along its surface, were thrown into the farthest corner of the mysterious temple.

Altars, altar steps, and niches were heavy with gold, the plaques of the precious metal being bound together by a wonderful cement. This hidden temple was, in a word, a veritable gold mine.

On the eastern wall was an image of the divinity, wrought in massive gold, and representing a human head surrounded by shafts of light. The heavy plaque was studded with emeralds and other precious stones. The rays of the rising sun fell full upon it, filling the whole temple with a light that seemed almost supernatural, and flashing back from the gold ornaments with which walls and vault were incrusted. Gold, in the poetic language of the country, was "the tears of the Sun," and the Temple blazed with the precious metal. The cornices crowning the sanctuary walls were also of gold, and a frieze of gold, hammered into the stone, ran right round the hall.

Raymond and Orellana, from their place of vantage, could see a number of chapels placed symmetrically round the great central chamber. One of them was sacred to the Moon, mother of the Incas. Her effigy was almost identical with that of the Sun, but the plaque was of silver, recalling the soft glow of that gentle world. Another chapel was dedicated to the Armies of the Heavens, which are the stars and the brilliant court of the sister of the Sun; a third, to thunder and lightning, the terrible ministers of her wrath; yet another, to the rainbow. And in all these chapels, as in the temple, all that was not silver was gold, gold, gold.

The young engineer's eyes gradually took in all the details of the temple. First, the central altar, several steps above the floor, on which were golden vases brimming over with maize, incense burners, ewers for the blood of the sacrifice, and a great golden knife on a tray of gold. Then he realized that something living was moving in the hall, which he had thought deserted. The Guardians of the Temple, like three hideous gnomes, glided from altar to altar, while the one with the cap skull, given the taste for blood from his earliest years by this deformation of the cranium, urged the others to hasten, and every little while went to the main altar to pat the great knife waiting there. Behind the altar, and rising above it, was a kind of golden pyramid, crowned with a golden throne.

"That is for the King," said Orellana.

On each side of the altar, and before it, were three other pyramids. But they were not so high, and were not of gold. They were of wood.

"The pyres," explained Orellana.

"The pyres! What do you mean?"

"Steady, steady! They're not going to burn her. She's the Bride of the Sun, and they wall her up. Burn her, indeed! It's not done, I tell you. Every Aïmara child knows that. Little children don't see the Temple of Death unless they are to die in it, but they know that much. Burn my daughter, indeed! As if I would allow it! What do you think I brought this pick for? You do just as well not to answer. Much better remain silent than talk nonsense like that. If you look at the walls out there, you'll see a big porphyry slab between each gold panel. There are just a hundred of them, and behind each one is one of the Sun's brides. If I only knew which tomb my daughter was in, I would have had her out a long time ago. But the slabs are all just alike, and there is nothing to help a poor father in his search. This time, though, I'm watching, and as soon as they've gone, I shall save her."

"She may be dead, smothered alive, when you get her out," whispered Raymond, against hope, thinking hard while the old man babbled on.

"That just shows how little you know about it. They are deep tombs, like cupboards, and you can sit in them. Don't you know the Indians always bury people sitting? There's air enough in there to keep her alive for an hour, or even two. And I shall have her out in ten minutes!"

Raymond stared blindly at the porphyry slabs before him.

"But if there are a hundred of them in there already, there isn't room for another. Are you sure?"

"Of course, I am. You needn't worry, boy. The pyres are for the two mammaconas who go before the Bride to prepare her chamber in the Enchanted Realm of the Sun."

"There are three pyres, though."

"Naturally. They have to take out the oldest bride to make room for my daughter. Then they burn her. What else should they do?"

"Burn her? Then they do burn her!"

Raymond had almost lost control of his mind.

"The old one, you fool!" retorted Orellana testily. "Didn't I tell you there were a hundred there? The Sun is given a new bride every ten years. Can you count, or can't you? That makes one of them a thousand years-old... There's no harm in burning a wife who is a thousand years-old. The Sun has got tired of her by then. Doesn't he set fire to her pyre himself? That proves it... Listen. Here they come!"

The chanting grew louder, and soon the priests appeared. Behind them walked the nobles, recognizable by the heavy ear-rings which only descendants of an Inca may wear; they were dressed in sleeveless red tunics, and each man bore a banner on which was embroidered a rainbow, its brilliant hues varying to mark the coat-armor of each house. Next came young girls of noble family, who in the old days would have become Brides of the Sun, ending their lives on the altars of the deity, or as the wives of the Inca. They were followed by their adult brothers, wearing the white robes, crosses embroidered on the breast, which were the traditional costume of men of their caste about to enter the order of knighthood. After them, the *curacas*, chiefs of the tribes conquered by the Incas and of all of these which had taken the oath of fealty. These men wore multi-colored tunics, unadorned with gold.

The cortège had advanced to the center of the temple, and suddenly, as the chanting ceased, all turned toward the door by which they had entered. A strange silence succeeded the rhythmic throbbing of canticles.

Then a terrible scream tore the air. Raymond gripped Orellana's arm.

"What was that?" he asked hoarsely.

"Nothing to do with us. They're sacrificing a child in the Black Chapel of Pacahuamac, the Pure Spirit."

CHAPTER II

"The devils!" Raymond wrenched out his revolver, but the old man gripped his wrist

"Quiet, you fool! We can't save the child now, and if you make a move, we shan't save her either. If you can't stand it, get out!"

The young engineer controlled himself.

"It's too horrible! Poor little Christobal! My God, why can't they kill us all and have done with it!"

"You should be ashamed of yourself, talking like that," said the madman. "When a man has nerves like a woman, he shouldn't come to the Temple of Death."

After that one terrible cry, all was silence again. Nobles, virgins, young men and *curacas* continued their slow progress round the Temple. Behind them entered the *amautas*, the sages who teach the children of the Incas; the Red Ponchos, who surrounded the altar like a sacred guard. None of them carried visible arms. The high dignitaries of the court followed, wearing the *blanchana*, a flowing tunic of light bark, painted in vivid colors. Each man carried a barbaric emblem with wide-open jaws, designed to frighten away all evil spirits.

Raymond thought that Marie-Thérèse was entering, but then saw that the litter borne on the shoulders of nobles was occupied by a figure which he did not at first recognize. His robe and sandals seemed of solid gold, and his ears were weighted down with enormous earrings, reaching almost to the shoulders. About his head was the royal *llantu*, a multi-colored turban of delicate tissue, and his forehead was further adorned by the kingly *borla*, the heavy scarlet and gold fringe of which partly hid his eyes. Two coraquenque plumes towered above the crown.

As he descended from his litter, aided by two pages, and slowly mounted the steps of the golden pyramid, the assembly bent to its knees. At the summit of the pyramid, he paused gravely, took his seat on the golden throne, and gave the Aimara greeting:

"*Dios anki tiourata.*"

Then all rose to their feet, while he sat motionless, like a graven image.

"The bank clerk!" exclaimed Raymond, as he faced toward the hidden watchers.

They had before them Huayna Capac Runtu, King of the Incas.

"The god is seated in all his light!" chanted the assembly in unison, repeating the words three times.

Then the wail of the *quenias* filled the air, and the religious cortège entered the temple, led by the four Guards of the Sacrifice, their heads erect now, for the sacred bonnets hid no secret. Behind them walked another Red Poncho, bearing in his hands a mass of knotted cords. Raymond recognized the Preacher of Cajamarca, head of the *quipucamyas*, or Keepers of the Historic Word. Then came Huascar, in the saffron-colored vestments of the high-priest, preceded by lesser dignitaries of the church, while four *curacas* held over him a canopy of brilliant-hued plumes. All bowed before Huascar; the Inca alone was above him.

From the high priest's stern face and somber eyes, Raymond looked to his hands, to see if they were red with the blood of sacrifice. He felt a wild desire to shoot him down there, to kill him like a mad dog among his priests and servitors.

The mammaconas advanced, chanting. He could not at first see Marie-Thérèse, hidden from view by black veils, rhythmically waved about her. The movement ceased and the women parted, leaving the way clear for the two among them who were to die and who advanced with uncovered faces, smiling like happy children.

The *quenias* ceased their song, and the second litter was brought forward in solemn silence. Raymond shivered. Was Marie-Thérèse dead or alive? He hoped vainly that her litter might pass close to him, as had Huascar's canopy. From where he was, she seemed as inert and lifeless as the mummy monarch beside her, and little Christobal was no longer in her arms. That part of her face left uncovered by the golden robe and head-dress was tomb-like in its pallor, and her eyes were closed.

The double throne was set down between the altar and the pyres; Huascar took his seat on the right of the altar, and the chief of the qui-pucamyas on the left; the mammaconas stood on the altar-steps. The two who were to die, their black veils discarded for dainty holiday attire, with flowers in their tresses, knelt at Marie-Thérèse's feet. The nobles and the curacas were ranged round the temple with the virgins and young men. The three Guardians of the Temple closed the doors. No others might enter, for the common people, forbidden the sight of these mysteries, waited far away, in the Corridors of Night, until the priests should return to lead them back through the labyrinth to the light of day.

Huascar rose, and his sonorous voice opened the ceremony.

"At the beginning was Pacahuamac, the Pure Spirit, who reigned in the darkness; then came his son, the Sun, and his daughter, the Moon; and Pacahuamac gave them armies, which are the Stars. Unto the Sun and Moon were born children. First were the Pirhuas, the pontiffs; then the Amautas, the kings; and then the Incas, kings of kings, sent on earth to rule mankind."

The assembly repeated Huascar's words like a litany. When it was ended, young men brought a llama to the altar, and the Guardians of the Temple offered up the sacrifice. Huascar bent over the entrails.

"The gods are propitious," he announced to the King.

At a sign from the throne, the chief of the *quipucamyas* rose to his feet, and in a few verses recalled the chief terrestrial episodes of the history of the Incas, the assembly chanting other verses in reply in the same monotonous rhythm, while the priest slipped the knots of the *quipus* through his fingers like a monk telling his beads.

When he reached the verse recounting Atahualpa's martyrdom, a great shout went up in the temple. The King, from his throne, raised a sceptered hand, and spoke. The end of the bondage placed upon his people by the gods was near; he, Huayna Capac Runtu, had been chosen by the Sun to drive out the strangers; and as a gage of his reconciliation with the faithful, the god had permitted them to offer him in sacrifice the noblest and most beautiful virgin of the hated race, a descendant of one of those who had murdered Atahualpa.

At the King's words, all eyes were carried to Marie-Thérèse, and a roar of "*Muera la Coya!*" beat round her. Was she not already dead, then? The savage cries did not even make her eyelids quiver. If she was still alive, she must be unconscious. Raymond, falling to his knees, thanked heaven for that.

Again the King's voice rose, telling the people that the day of deliverance was near; that their empire would be reborn in all its splendor. The altars of their god, served for centuries in the darkness, would soon smoke anew in his light. Once again would they be the Free Children of the Sun.

"Let the Children of the Sun advance!"

The young men approached the royal throne. For thirty days they had gone through the tests of yore; they had fasted, fought, displayed their skill in wrestling and with arms; they had worn coarse clothing, walked barefoot, and slept on the hard floor. Now they advanced in their white robes, the cross on their breasts, like young knights of the Middle Ages in the Gothic cathedrals of another faith and land.

They surrounded the golden pyramid and Huascar, taking evergreen branches from a golden vase held by two virgins, bound them in their hair as a sign that the virtues they had acquired must last for all time. Then, one by one, he called their names to the King, who, as each young man knelt before him, pierced his ears with a golden awl. They descended, their white robes smeared with blood, while Huascar, from another vase, took heavy ear-rings, with which he adorned them. Nothing in the young faces betrayed their suffering. Then all raised their hands and took the oath of bravery and of fealty to the Inca.

"That is well," said the King. "Let them now put on their sandals."

This part of the ceremony was performed by the quipucamyas, the most venerable among them strapping on the young men's feet the sandals of the Order of the Incas.

"That is well," repeated the King. "Let them be given their girdles."

Again the old men passed down the ranks, buckling on the heavy war-belts.

"That is well," said the King for the third time. "And I say unto you before the dead King and the Goya who is to die, that they may repeat it to your ancestors, that our race is still the first of all living races, for you are the pure Children of the Sun, without earthly leaven, the brother having always drunk the blood of the sister!"

The virgins advanced, taking the places of the young men on the steps of the throne, while fathers and brothers intoned the Aïmara Song of Triumph.

"The savages! The savages!" raged Raymond, thinking only of vengeance now that he thought Marie-Thérèse was dead. He balanced the revolver in his palm, hesitating. There were at all events Huascar and the King he could bring down; that would be some satisfaction. But suppose Marie-Thérèse was not dead after all? He might still save her. For a moment he thought she had moved. He questioned Orellana in a whisper.

"My daughter is very tired, and must be sleeping," replied the madman.

Meanwhile, the cap-skulled Guardian of the Temple had made a little incision on the throat of each virgin, gathering their blood in a gold ewer. When the cup was full, he touched it with his lips and handed it to the young men, among whom it passed from hand to hand, while the girls, proud of their light wounds, cried,:

"Glory to the Children of the Sun!"

"The cup is empty," announced Huascar.

At his words the King rose, and holding up both arms to the heavens, implored the Sun to give the signal for the sacrifice. Clouds of pungent incense rose from the burners, and gradually hid from view the azure disc overhead. The mammaconas who were to die, obeying the ritual, ran forward to the King's feet.

"We implore you, O King, to stop all the smokes of the earth. They hide his face, and the Sun cannot give the signal for the sacrifice."

At a sign from the figure on the golden pyramid, the burners were extinguished, and the spot of blue gradually reappeared. The Guardians of the Temple, by the pyres, held in their hands metal mirrors, drawing the sun to a little heap of cotton in the center of each resinous pile. Thus did the god, of his own will, give the signal for the sacrifice! There were no stakes on the pyres, no chains; the victims must die willingly.

While the throng about them chanted prayers, the two mammaconas watched the pyres. They feared that the god might reject them; then they would live, shunned by all, until they disappeared. Their eyes, large with hope in the mercy of the divinity, anxiously awaited the first flicker of flame.

If the pyre destined to the thousand-year-old Coya did not take fire, it did not mean that the new one was distasteful to the god. It meant merely that the old one had not known how to please him, that she was not worthy of the sepulcher of fire, and that her body must be thrown to the black vultures in the mountains.

On this day, the first pyre to blaze up was that of the long-dead Coya. She was waiting. Songs rang out in her honor, and a purple veil which Raymond had not yet noticed fell to the ground. A black gap showed in the wall, and in it could be seen the shadowy figure of the thousand year-old queen, stiff in her scented wrappings.

CHAPTER III

Raymond's head swam. There, before him, was the narrow tomb into which Marie-Thérèse would be buried alive. But was she still alive? She must have died when the child was torn from her arms, or when she had heard his terrible cry.

The priests had lifted the dead Coya from her tomb, and carried her to the pyre. She sat severely erect, as Coyas should sit, even when slowly done to death in a living tomb. So she must sit, and that is why the tomb is made so narrow that she can only remain motionless on her throne. Erect and calm, she vanished in the flames of the pyre, while the two living mammaconas watched her enviously.

Raymond did not even glance at the pyres. His eyes were fixed on the hole in the wall. She could not live long in there, and they must lose no time if she was to be saved. One hand gripped Orellana's pick, while the other, armed with a revolver, still hesitated. Perhaps Marie-Thérèse was not dead yet! But, if so why did she not open her eyes?

Still the two other pyres did not take fire, and the mammaconas prayed passionately to the Sun. They must die before Marie-Thérèse, to prepare her chamber in the Enchanted Realms of the Sun, and if they did not hasten they would never reach them first.

"Have pity, O Sun! Send us your flames, Ejma of the Heavens! We are women; give us courage."

"Have pity! Send us your flames!" chanted the throng in unison.

But the Sun did not send his flame until the first pyre had nearly died down, its end hastened by the perfumes heavy with spirit which the Guards of the Sacrifice poured over the blazing logs.

Dropping their festive garments from them, the two mammaconas ran to the pyres with cries of joy, and waited, their eyes turned heavenwards in ecstasy. Diabolical music burst out about them, and a savage frenzy seemed to seize the other mammaconas as they whirled round the fires. The greedy flames climbed upwards and reached the victims. One of them leaped down with a terrible cry.

"Return to the flames! Return to the flames!" chanted the others, surrounding her.

She writhed on the ground, calling for the knife, and a Guardian of the Temple went toward her. The black veils of the mammaconas were spotted with blood, but they danced on, singing. The hideous dwarfs lifted up a body, which disappeared in the fire.

The other mammacona, heroically erect, had cried out only once, and when she in her turn vanished in the scarlet chariot which the Sun had sent to take her to his Enchanted Realm, hymns of glory thundered through the temple.

Maddened by the songs, the flames, the incense, and the acrid smoke of the pyres, three more mammaconas followed their sisters. It is impossible to guess how far this delirium of sacrifice would have gone had not Huascar stopped it. At a sign from him, the diabolical music ceased, and the Guardians of the Temple choked the glowing pyres with sand.

It was Marie-Thérèse's turn. Raymond, half fainting, opened his eyes again at Orellana's words. He saw the mammaconas strip her of the jewels with which she was literally covered from head to foot. From her hair, ears, cheeks, breast, shoulders, from her beautiful arms and shapely ankles, the "tears of the Sun" fell one by one, and were placed preciously in a golden basin. Last of all they removed the fatal Golden Sun bracelet All these jewels were to be hidden again until the day, ten years thence, when the Inca would demand another bride for the Sun.

As she was rapidly divested of her golden sheath as well, Marie-Thérèse appeared swathed in bands of soft material. Her eyes were closed, and externally at all events, she was already a mummy. Her arms were bound to her sides, and all that remained to be done was to lift her into her tomb. Raymond's eyes did not leave what could still be seen of the beloved face under the bands of perfumed linen which bound her chin and forehead. Her lips were parted, but motionless, as if she had just breathed her last sigh.

Again he told himself that she must be dead. It was better so, for then she could not feel the hands of the horrible Guardians of the Temple lift her to the death-throne and then slide her into the hole where she was to wait a thousand years before being burned in her turn.

At that moment, the rays of the Sun, as if to make a golden ladder for the woman whom the Incas, in their cruel piety, were sending to his realms, fell on Marie-Thérèse, and lit up the narrow tomb, so that Raymond saw every detail of the atrocious ceremony.

The three porphyry slabs, fitting perfectly one into the other, had now to be adjusted, and the tomb would be closed. It was done in terrible-silence, and all eyes were fixed on workers and victim.

Bending under its weight, the Guardians of the Temple slipped the first into position, hiding Marie-

Thérèse up to the knees. The second, brought to the right level on a rolling platform, covered her to the shoulders.

All that could now be seen was her head, swathed and bound up for the thousand-year sleep, with a face that was that of a dead woman. Then a shiver ran through the throng, though it had witnessed the sacred horrors preceding it without a quiver. Marie-Thérèse had opened her eyes...

They had opened wide and stared out from the depths of the tomb which was closing on her. They were terribly living, terribly wide open, staring, staring, at all she would see of life before the eternal Shadow took her to its bosom. And those eyes traveled slowly over the throng in gala attire which was there to see her die, then rested for the last time on the golden sunlight, on the beautiful light of day.

The superhuman agony forced those eyes even wider, those eyes which were never to see again. Her lips moved, as if about to utter a supreme cry of appeal to life, a cry of horror at the living night of the tomb. Then they closed again on a poor, weak little groan, while the last slab blotted out the look of those great eyes.

She belonged to the god now.

CHAPTER IV

Huascar raised his hand, and the temple began to empty in silence. There was not a song, not a murmur, only the slip of innumerable sandals on the stone slabs of the floor. Huascar and his priests, the nobles, young men, virgins, curacas and mammaconas crossed the threshold of the golden doors.

Huayna Capac Runtu had descended from his throne and taken his seat beside the dead King, on the seat left vacant by Marie-Thérèse; the Red Ponchos lifted the two monarchs, the dead, and the living, to their shoulders, and in their turn vanished into the Corridor of Night.

There remained in the hall only the Guardians of the Temple and the ashes of the first victims.

Hardly had the three gnomes closed the doors to carry out their horrible duties in peace than a shadow rose up before them. Squeaking with terror, they fled into the Chapel of the Moon, but vengeance followed them there, and it was at the foot of its altar that they were shot down like loathsome beasts. White as Marie-Thérèse had been, but icy-cool in the moment of action, Raymond fired only one shot into each hideous skull.

Then he turned and ran into the temple, where Orellana was already raining blows on the tomb with his pick. Raymond wrenched the tool from his hands, and set to work. But the stones did not move. His forehead covered with icy perspiration, he forced himself to think, to reason, trying to forget Marie-Thérèse in her tomb and bring his engineer's knowledge to bear on the problem.

Those stones could not be very heavy. Orellana and he could lift them easily if the three dwarfs could. They were evidently made light so that they could be readily removed by the priests at certain ceremonies. But what, was their secret? What was their secret?

Quelling the moral storm that would have sent him raging impotently against this rampart, he compelled himself to look for the jointing of the stones. His hands were trembling, so he stopped for a minute to control himself, and then tried again. Again he failed. How were they moved?

He had seen them put back into position before his eyes, so there had to be a way. But where was he to press, where strike? And meanwhile Marie-Thérèse was dying behind those stones! Dying!

Again he raised the pick, whirled it over his head, and struck at random, on the left side of the stone. Every ounce of his strength, doubled by despair, had been put into that blow, and the slab turned slightly on itself, to the right. The socket in which the stones rested was so made that they could swing and slip out of their frame on that side. With a shout of triumph, he swung the pick over his head.

"Marie-Thérèse! Marie-Thérèse!"

Behind him, the madman was calling too.

"Maria Cristina! Maria Cristina!"

Raymond was still raining blows on the slab. Soon it had turned so far that he could catch hold of it with his hands, and tore them in a vain effort to hasten. With the handle of the pick he pushed on the left again, and the stone came half out of its socket.

This time, both he and Orellana could get firm hold and put their strength into it. The stone yielded, came toward them.

"Marie-Thérèse! Marie-Thérèse!"

One more effort and she would be free.

A prodigious heave, a struggle with teeth set and breath whistling, and the slab came away altogether, thundered on the floor as Raymond hurled it from off his shoulder.

"Marie-Thérèse!"

There was no answer from the tightly-bound head dimly visible in the darkness. He leaned forward.

"My God. It's not Marie-Thérèse!"

CHAPTER V

Turning from the century-dead Coya with an inarticulate cry of rage, Raymond seized Orellana by the throat as if he would have strangled the poor madman, who had started work on the wrong tomb. And he, thrice accursed fool that he was, had followed the madman's lead, made a mistake when every minute might mean Marie-Thérèse's life!

And now, which was it? The tomb on the right or that on the left? Or neither?

Losing the old man, he controlled himself again by a superhuman effort and looked round the temple. No, there could be no mistake this time. It must be the one on the right. He looked for the angle from their hiding-place to the altar. Yes, this was the one!

The pick thundered on another slab, while Orellana, a raving maniac now, danced and gibbered behind him, grunting with every blow as if he himself had delivered it.

At last the stone turned... It moved... slid into their arms... fell to the ground.

"Marie-Thérèse! It is I, Raymond! For God's sake, speak!"

Again he bent over the rigid face of a long-forgotten Coya.

Raymond fell to the ground as if stunned. But Orellana was already at work again, setting him the example, and the young engineer was on his feet in a moment. It had to be that other one on the left, then!

Once again he wrenched the pick from the old man's feeble hands and hammered on the granite... The minutes were flying... flying. And she may be dying behind that slab, struggling for breath!... The thunder of blows echoed through the hall... the stone moved... slipped... fell... At last... No!... Another dead woman... Another, another!... Not Marie-Thérèse!

"Maria Cristina! My daughter! Dearest, I am coming! Your father is here!"

While Raymond staggered to the wall, staring before him with blind eyes, the old man, peering into the tomb, had recognized his child.

"Maria Cristina! Dearest! Wait, wait! Only one more stone, and you will be out of your prison!"

Sobbing and laughing in turn, Orellana worked desperately, finding the strength of his youth anew.

Then Raymond fell on him.

"Give me that pick. You're wasting time on a dead woman. Give it to me, I say!"

There was a terrible struggle between the two, and Raymond, triumphant, whirled the tool over his head at another tomb, while Orellana, by the last effort of his life, tore the second stone from its socket, drew the dead body of his daughter to him and covered it with kisses and tears. Old madman and dead girl fell to the floor together.

Orellana was dead, but he had found his daughter.

Raymond saw and heard nothing. Another tomb open... and another dead Coya of long ago... The gods of the Temple of Death were ready to give up their dead, but not their living bride...

Crying, calling, driving his nails into his bleeding palms; ready to offer himself up to the ferocious spirit that guarded those tombs, Raymond staggered, fell, and got up again, dragging behind him the pick, which he no longer knew where to use, striving to reason and understand.

There was nothing here to help him! His eyes wandered hopelessly round the circular temple, trying to find a guiding point. Nothing! Perhaps chance would give him what his reasoning had failed to secure... Yes, that was it... why not try here?... It might be this tomb as well as any other... He set to work again, but heavily... oh, so heavily... and the pick weighed down his hands terribly.

Exhausted, he dropped it... He could do no more... And she was dying... dying... while the dead, torn from their eternal sleep, stared back at him with unseeing eyes.

How many hours had he been toiling? He did not know. The oblique rays of the sun had gradually risen on the walls, then vanished.

Then the light which succeeded them faded in its turn... Twilight had fallen... then darkness had come.

Stretched out on the altar steps, whither he had dragged himself with his last remaining strength, he closed his eyes and waited... waited for sleep or death.

What did it matter, since Marie-Thérèse was dead?

CHAPTER VI

One morning, as the little steamboat which ran between the Island of Titicaca and the mainland, was plowing its way through the waters of the lake, it was hailed by a tall Quichua Indian, standing upright in his pirogue. In the bottom of the frail craft lay a white man, and the captain, seeing the prostrate figure, hove to for a moment to pick it up. Thus did Raymond Ozoux return to civilization.

Among the passengers of the *Yavari* was a good-hearted alpaca merchant of Punho who took pity on the fever-stricken stranger and had him removed to his own home, where the whole household devoted itself to nursing the young man back to life. The Indian who brought him to the steamer explained that he had found the stranger, probably some tourist, unconscious among the ruins of the sacred island. He had therefore dosed him with pink water for the fever, and had brought him back to people of his own race. The Indian refused all reward, and the captain was the more surprised at this when, on searching Raymond, he found a considerable sum of money in his pockets. For a Quichua not to strip a helpless man was indeed remarkable.

When Raymond had sufficiently recovered to understand what was being said, he immediately recognized the Indian described to him as Huascar. In his quality as high-priest, Huascar had probably returned to the temple late at night, and there, had found Raymond, surrounded by gaping tombs, and the corpses of Orellana and the three Guardians of the Temple. Coldly calculating in his hatred, the Indian had decided to inflict the worst possible torture on Raymond, leaving him to live after the death of Marie-Thérèse.

That torture would not last long, the young man decided. The idea that he might have saved Marie-Thérèse had he not lost his head, and that her death lay at his door, tormented him without ceasing. He realized that he would never be able to free himself of this obsession and that it would finally drive him mad. Better to end it all at once.

Only he did not wish to die among these awful mountains, mute witnesses of the horrors that had cost him his self-respect and happiness. The Marie-Thérèse who was constantly before his mind's eye was not the terrible mummy-like figure he had last seen, but the dainty silhouette in the homely surroundings of the office at Callao, among the big green registers, where they had met again after so long an absence and where they had exchanged words of love. He would go there to rejoin her.

Once this decision was taken, he grew rapidly better, and one day, after warmly thanking his host and showering presents on the whole family, he took the train to Mollendo, where he would join some ship for Callao. The voyage seemed an interminable one. At Arequipa, he visited the little adobe house by the rio de Chili, and thought of the vain appeal they had made to that scoundrel Garcia. There also, for the first time since his illness, he thought of his traveling companions.

What had happened to Uncle François, Don Christobal and Natividad? Perhaps their bones were then bleaching in some inaccessible corner of the Corridors of Night. The Marquis, at all events, had not endured the torture of impotently witnessing the murder of his two children.

When Raymond reached Mollendo there was a howling gale on, but he at once went down to the harbor. It was deserted save for two shadows, which rushed toward him with cries of joy. Yes, they were alive and breathing: Uncle François and Natividad!

Though white and sad-looking, they did not seem to have suffered a great deal. Raymond clasped their hands, and they, seeing him so pale and thin, said no word.

Together they walked along for a few minutes, deep in thoughts. At last Monsieur Ozoux turned to his nephew:

"What happened to Don Christobal? Do you know?"

"I thought he was with you." Raymond's voice was toneless, detached from all things of this world.

It was only then that Natividad, without being asked, explained how he and Uncle François, after the frustrated attempt in the House of the Serpent, had been thrown into a dungeon in which they passed four days, and in which the illustrious scientist had at last become convinced of the reality of their adventure. At the end of those four days, finding the prison doors open and unguarded, they had fled.

Apparently all the Indians were bolting to the mountains from Cuzco, and the explanation for this they had found on reaching Sicuani. President Vointemilla, risking his all on one bold stroke, had surprised Garcia's forces in the middle of the Interaymi *fêtes*, and the four squadrons of his escort which remained faithful had cut up and routed the thousands of Quichua riflemen. Barely five hundred in all, but of Spanish blood, they had repeated Pizarro's exploit on those same plains of Xauxa, while the same ancient walls, with the impassability of immortal things, again stared down on the struggle of the races.

Garcia had escaped over the Bolivian frontier, and was on the point of blowing out his brains when he heard of a revolution in Paraguay which made life worth living again. So he crossed into Paraguay with his lawless "cabinet," to the great satisfaction of the President of Bolivia.

From Sicuani, Uncle François and Natividad had gone straight to Mollendo, hoping to find the Marquis there, if the new fortunes of the republic had also opened the doors of his prison. As to Raymond, they had not expected to see him until Lima, "after he had done everything to save Marie-Thérèse."

It was the first time that they had pronounced her name before him, and Raymond saw a very real and very great sympathy in their faces.

"She is dead," he said, gripping his uncle's shoulder.

"Poor boy!"

They paced up and down again, silently, before the raging breakers of the Pacific, which had already kept two of them prisoners in Mollendo for the past ten days. Raymond would not say another word, and his companions, ignorant of what had happened, could not even try to give him hope.

Eight more days passed by, and the elements still held them prisoners at Mollendo. His uncle and Natividad watched Raymond closely, but his outward calm finally dispelled their fears, and once aboard a ship for Callao, they even questioned him. He told them what he had seen in the Temple of Death, while they listened in horror to the simply-worded narrative, made in a singularly quiet voice. Afterwards, Uncle François locked himself in his cabin and sat for a long time with his head between his hands, staring at an unopened notebook.

Raymond, leaning over the ship's side, was now gazing idly at the rapidly approaching coast on which he had landed with so much hope and joy. The Peru of Pizarro and the Incas, the fabulous land of gold and legends, the Eldorado of his young ambition and of his love! Dead were his love and his ambition. There lived only the legends, at which they had laughed, which had killed all their dreams and which was to kill him after sending Marie-Thérèse to a living tomb! And they had laughed, laughed at the warning of those two stately old ladies, Velasquez canvases brought to life and striving to retain all their pictorial dignity!

As on that first day, he was the first man off the liner, dropping over the side into the swaying craft of a noisy boatman. This time, though, he did not need to ask where the Calle de Lima lay, and his eyes hardly left the part of the city to which he had hastened so full of hope, where Marie-Thérèse had waited for him.

He did not hurry on reaching land. Walking slowly he entered the network of tortuous streets, passed through the labyrinth of alleys, and finally reached the point whence he could see the veranda... There he had come to greet her every night, there he had come one night to find her gone. Never again would he see that dear face, that dainty figure bent over the big green books, while the slim fingers toyed with a golden pencil attached to her supple waist with a long gold chain.

Suddenly Raymond stopped, staggered, and put his hand to his side with a choking intake of breath... It hurt, that hallucinating apparition on the veranda... Or perhaps it is true that the shades of the dear departed come back to people the spots they loved best, that they have the power of showing themselves to those they loved... For Marie-Thérèse was there, leaning out as she used to, turning her sweet face as she used to... How pale she was, how diaphanous; her well-remembered gestures were no more than the ghosts of those gestures!

He hardly dared breathe, fearing that the vision would vanish at the sound of his voice... He advanced cautiously, stealthily, like a child stalking a butterfly.

"Raymond!"

"Marie-Thérèse!"

They fell in each other's arms. The cry which had come from those pale lips was a living one. They clung to each other, trembling, laughing, crying, and would have fallen in their weakness had not other shadows come to their aid.

Aunt Agnes and her duenna, Irene, held up Marie-Thérèse, while Don Christobal, running out into the street, caught the young engineer under the arm, and led him slowly in.

Little Christobal, dancing at the door of the office, shouted with glee and clapped his hands together.

"I told you so, Marie-Thérèse! I told you he wasn't dead! Now you'll get better, Marie-Thérèse!"

Marie-Thérèse, in Raymond's arms again, was sobbing.

"I knew you would come back here if you were still alive... But is it really you, Raymond?... Really you?"

"Marie-Thérèse has been awfully ill," explained the child, while the two old ladies cried. "But we cured her by telling her you were not dead. Of course I knew Huascar had saved you too... Huascar saved us all, you know... He took us away from all those nasty Indians... And father said that we would all be dead, but for him.

Didn't you, Father? But now you mustn't die anymore, must you?"

"I was there, Marie-Thérèse. I saw them put you into the tomb."

"You were there, then! I knew it. I felt your eyes on mine, and that's why I looked. I knew you were watching... somewhere... When they took Christobal away from me, I thought I would die... Huascar had told me he would be quite safe, but I couldn't believe it... Then that horrible cry!... I didn't open my eyes again until I felt yours on them... I knew you were there, my darling."

The two old ladies and the Marquis were making desperate signs to him, and Raymond tried to stop her, but she went on:

"I knew you wouldn't leave me there to die, and so I waited, waited... It was terribly long... And then I began to choke... I couldn't move; only sit there and wait... What does it matter, Father, now that we're all alive and happy? Then I heard somebody thundering blows on the wall, and thought you were coming... Only just in time, for I was choking... There was such funny music in my ears... Then I heard the stone torn away, and felt myself being lifted out... When I opened my eyes, Raymond, it was not you, but Huascar... He carried me into a dark little room, with a torch burning in it, and untied my arms and head... Then he slipped on that horrible bat-skin dress again... I couldn't believe I was saved, though he told me so..."

She paused for a moment, choking, and continued:

"He left me where I was, and started working. First he lifted a mummy into my place. 'There is no sacrilege,' he said, 'for the god now has the number of wives he needs.' He had evidently prepared everything, and dug an opening as deep into the back of my tomb as he dared... I was horribly afraid, because he said he had done it all for love of me... and I screamed when he tried to pick me up... I was ever so much more afraid than in the tomb... He laughed, and said I was lucky to have had him for a friend... You, he said, had nearly spoiled his plans, and he had had to trap you all to save me.

"When I told him that he had only saved me for a worse fate, he laughed again... Then he picked me up, for I was too weak to move, and carried me miles and miles through the darkness... When he stopped, it was before a low door... He pushed it open, and there were father and Christobal... While they were kissing me, Huascar went to the door... He looked awful... Then he said to father: 'Señor, I promised to return your son and daughter to you. Here they both are. You will find nothing to prevent your departure. An Inca, señor, never breaks his word.' We have not seen him since... I had to tell you, Raymond, so that if ever you meet that man again, you will know what we owe him."

At her last words, the young engineer shivered and pressed her hand.

"He need not be afraid. I remember what I owe him. He saved both of you and us, darling, and I promised him that if he saved you..."

"I know, I know! Father has told me..."

"He considered your promise an insult," interrupted the Marquis. "After my capture, they took me to the Island, and he came to see me in my dungeon. I thought my last hour had come, and did not spare him with my tongue. He let me finish, and then explained what he had done, his whole plan of action. When Marie-Thérèse and Christobal were brought to me, the two Indians guarding my door, who were his absolute slaves, would take us both to the mainland in a pirogue. He told me, too, of your interview at Arequipa, and gave me a message for you. Here it is:

" 'Tell that young man, whom I do not know, that the señorita will be as free as her heart, which is neither mine to take, to buy or to sell. He must know that. I have done him no harm, and he has insulted me. But I forgive him.' Then, as he was about to go, he turned again: and said:

" 'Do not thank me, señor. Thank the one who is now in heaven, and who was the señora de la Torre. I ask for only one thing in exchange for my services, and that is for you never to speak of them. The memory of the High Priest of the Incas must not be dishonored.'

"That is Huascar's message, Raymond. There is no reason why you should not marry Marie-Thérèse."

At this moment, Uncle François and Natividad dashed into the room. On their way from the harbor, they had learned of the Marquis' miraculous return to Lima with his two children, and hearing that the whole family had come to Callao that day—Marie-Thérèse to see her dear old office for the last time!—they had come there running. Aunt Agnes and Irene, anxious for their charge's health, would have taken her away, but the young girl insisted that this storm of still shaky laughter and interjections was the best medicine for her malady.

"It's all a bad dream," she said. "That is how we must take it."

Don Christobal took up the cue.

"Exactly. I have had a long talk with Vointemilla, and that is the way he asks us to treat it, for patriotic reasons. In exchange, he has promised to help me wind up the business here and sell our concessions. Raymond and Marie-Thérèse will be married in France, if nobody objects."

222

Natividad alone had objections to make, and waved his arms disconsolately above his head.

"The same old story!" he groaned. "If I had my way, we should soon get to the bottom of those Corridor of Night mysteries... But no! The same old game of shut your eyes and see nothing... Here's Vointemilla now, instead of settling with those Indians once and for all, asking us to call it a bad dream! Bad dream indeed!"

"My dear Natividad," said the Marquis. "I fear you are a troubled spirit. By the way, I have sad news for you. You are no longer the Chief of Police of Callao."

Natividad fell into a chair, his mouth wide open, struggling for words to qualify the airy attitude of this man, for whom he had risked everything. He was so comical that they all burst into laughter, while the little old gentleman, purple with fury, strode toward the door.

"Not so quick, Natividad, not so quick!" called the Marquis after him. "There is also some good news for you. You have been appointed Chief of Police in Lima."

Again Natividad fell into a chair, but this time, beaming, stuttering with joy and gratitude.

"It's a dream... the dream of my life... I might have been dead though!"

"The appointment, which I saw President Vointemilla sign, is, of course, only valid in the event of your being alive," smiled the Marquis. "As those Indians of yours haven't eaten you alive, you can keep an eye on them again."

"Hush! We must not talk about it," replied Natividad, the magistrate's toga weighing on his shoulders again.

"And neither shall we," whispered Raymond, bending over Marie-Thérèse's pale face.

She nodded slowly.

"Do you know, Raymond, looking around me and seeing the same old chairs and books again, the same dear faces, and when I think of the Temple of Death, it really does only seem like an ugly dream."

Natividad, having said good bye to all, was talking to the Marquis by the door. He opened it and fell back with a muffled exclamation.

A corpse, until then held upright by the closed door, fell into the room.

Marie-Thérèse, first to realize who it was, fell on her knees beside the body.

It was Huascar, whom she had driven out of that door, who had dragged himself there to die, a dagger in his heart.

EPILOGUE

This story must have an epilogue, for I have not yet had occasion to speak again of Oviedo Runtu, bank clerk and last King of the Incas. After a thousand adventures in the Andes, which I may describe to you some day, Oviedo Runtu and his lieutenants in the revolt with Garcia were tracked down by Natividad's police.

Oviedo Runtu surrendered and saved his life by promising to quench the last embers of revolt. Tried by court-martial, he was sentenced to perpetual exile, but Natividad subsequently interceded and obtained his pardon. It was, moreover, the new Chief of Police of Lima who secured him a post at Punho, in a branch of the Franco-Belgian bank. There Natividad could watch him, and finally convinced himself that the bank clerk-King did nothing to resuscitate the marvelous *fêtes* of the Interaymi.

Oviedo Runtu died very prosaically, after marrying a lady of Lima who had made the trip to Lake Titicaca especially to see the last King of the Incas. Of that journey was born a romance, and for years, travelers passing through Punho thereafter would have the royal couple pointed out to them. They were always very much amused when they heard that the King, working daily in a bank, earned just one hundred' and fifty *soles* a month.

One day, when some charitable souls were chaffing the King's widow about the mediocre state in which she lived, the Coya, as she was derisively called, retorted that had she and her husband so wished, they could have been the wealthiest couple on earth. But the treasures of the Incas, she added, belonged to the gods and the dead, and none might touch them.

Asked if she had ever seen those treasures, the Coya asserted that her husband had shown them to her once, and she told fabulous stories of the riches hidden in the Temple of Death. Naturally, nobody believed her.[3]

Even so, none believed the soldiers of Pizarro when they said that in Peru, their horses had been shod with silver!

---

[3] The anonymous author of the book *Antiy y monumentos del Peru* adds: "It is widely known, and generally admitted, that there exists in the ancient fortress of the Cuzco a secret room In which is hidden a vast treasure, consisting chiefly of golden statues of all the Incas. A lady who has been in this room is still living. This is Doña Maria de Esquivel, wife of the last Inca. I have heard her tell how she was taken there. Don Carlos, husband of this lady, did not live in a manner suited to his rank, and she often upbraided him, saying that she had been cozened into marrying a poor Indian under the pompous style of 'Lord of the Incas.' She said this so often that Don Carlos grew angry, and one day retorted: 'Madam, I will show you whether I am rich or poor. Too will see that no lord, no monarch on this earth, has a greater treasure than I.' Taking her to the ruined fortress, he bound her eyes, and led her only a few steps before removing the bandage again. She was in a great quadrangular hall, and ranged all about it were the statues of the Incas, each about the size of a twelve-year-old child, and all of massive gold. She saw also many vases of gold and silver, the whole making one of the most magnificent treasures in the world."